Camille in October

THE PRIDE LIST

Camille in October

MIREILLE BEST

TRANSLATED BY STEPHANIE SCHECHNER

LONDON NEW YORK CALCUTTA

THE PRIDE LIST

EDITED BY SANDIP ROY AND BISHAN SAMADDAR

The Pride List presents new as well as classic works of queer literature to the world. An eclectic collection of books of queer stories, biographies, histories, thoughts, ideas, experiences and explorations, the Pride List does not focus on any specific region, nor on any specific genre, but celebrates the fantastic diversity of LGBTQ+ lives across countries, languages, centuries and identities, with the conviction that queer pride comes from its unabashed expression.

www.bibliofrance.in

The work is published with the support of the
Publication Assistance Programmes of the Institut français

Seagull Books, 2019

Originally published in French as *Camille en octobre*

First published in English translation by Seagull Books, 2019

ISBN 978 0 8574 2 697 0

British Library Cataloguing-in-Publication Data
A catalogue record for this book is available from the British Library

Typeset by Seagull Books, Calcutta, India
Printed and bound by Versa Press, East Peoria, Illinois, USA

. . . And Yahweh says to Cain: 'Where is Abel, your brother?' He replies: 'I don't know; am I my brother's keeper?' . . .

I

'Where now? When now? Who now?'

S. Beckett (*The Unnamable* 3)[1]

Now the wind has died down. The street is dizzyingly empty. It's a weekday, in October. It's four in the afternoon. The hour of nothingness. The hour when the Mothers drink coffee during lulls in the conversation. The hour when one feels absolutely adrift   Without the men   Without the kids   Without anything that would force you to function. If the Mothers were able to name this full-body turmoil, this desolate wandering of an unoccupied spirit, this uselessness of limbs that renders them inert and numb, if the Mothers killed themselves, it would be on a weekday In October   In the middle of the afternoon.

1 Samuel Beckett, *The Unnamable* (New York: Grove Press, 1958). All quotations from this text are from this edition.

But the Mothers in the neighbourhood commit suicide rarely, that's a fact. They listen to the radio Flip through their magazines They quietly go gaga between the hit songs and the knitting the dread of meals and the money troubles They stack the old clothes in order of size, badly mend the holes, cook things, scrub others, wash everything that can stand up to water clean the rest and tidy up all that eternally drags and overflows and threatens to submerge them. And as soon as this anxiety comes upon them, they quickly flee to gather, with their idle hands wrapped around the warmth of the cups, to listen to the same old stories, which vary sometimes but just barely, ignorant of the fact that this thing they must escape has a name. They endure. The world is dismal and blurry. The urgent need to keep on living pushes them to these pathetic feelings of animosity To a burst of laughter To the desire to drink something hot.

Ariane Abel and me, we were there. Among them. In the middle. Everywhere. Almost transparent. Little glass animal figurines which they bumped up against by accident And what are you doing there, huh? Suddenly, this place was no longer ours. We would have to meet up elsewhere, but where? The kids spent their time getting caught red-handed And double-parked To be displaced pushed put out. Remembered only when absent—WHERE had you gone?—As though one passed through walls Slithered underground Swam the river upstream—It's been hours that I've been looking for you, do you do it on purpose? —Dispersed under the cinders Evaporated between the mesh of the screens Disappeared Nowhere to be found.

They're crazy, Ariane always said to me. Completely nuts. Ariane was always tough, or rather compact, like a pebble: something that's seemingly smooth, slightly rough to the touch. Completely nuts, Ariane always said, completely.

Me, I was suspended in the atmosphere, participating in all realms. Endlessly permeable, I drifted, moved about like a fog. I was one or the other or everyone together, incapable of locating myself with certainty. I never really knew WHO I was. I don't even know if this is a thing that gets better with time, or if I will never do anything besides wandering between contradictory solidarities, with bouts of intense haste when I become a pebble, a shell against the pain, an instrument of hatred.

Abel was not made of volatile material, but was rather porous and spongy and went to pieces unexpectedly. He never had any opinion. But he too traversed zones of phenomenal pressure that transformed him briefly into explosive material.

All things considered, we were ordinary children, among the ordinary crazies who populated the neighbourhood. Folks patted us in passing Sometimes they said you're getting big Most often they showed us the tolerance universally offered around here to dogs cats drunks and bad weather, all things that you couldn't really tell if they were good or bad but which you had learnt to live with.

Now the wind has died down. The dead leaves have stopped crackling in the gutters where they ended up. Somewhere in an unseen street nearby, a maniac is setting off the car alarm, almost exactly every twenty-five seconds. It is a few minutes past four in the afternoon, on a weekday, in October. I finally got up from my chair, tore myself away from my dazed contemplation of the street, and had a plan: to call Ariane.

Ariane, and not my mother, whom I could reach in a few minutes; nor even Clara, who hasn't yet left the city. No. I'm going to call my little sister Ariane who is more than a thousand kilometres away. And even if she truly were on the other side of the Earth, as will surely happen with her, it's still her that I would call, there, now, in a state of urgency so painful that it wrings my heart like a cramp—without a thought about time zones that scramble time Without giving a thought to dragging her out of sleep or lovemaking. Ariane. Ariane. Abel is dead.

Oh my God, my mother had said Take care of your brother and your sister, I am going to see what . . . I went into Abel's room where the two little ones were curled up. My father is dead, I just killed him.

Abel is stiff like a pylon, his clear eyes piercing his head like fixed rays that drive through space through walls through skulls. From one moment to the next, stricken by his own radiance, he'll throw a fit, drop to the ground with a loud noise of bones cracking, his eyes finally rolling back inside his head and seeing nothing but that minuscule zone that has been roasted by short-circuiting and which is now smoking.

—With what? inquires Ariane who is always worried about insignificant details.

—With the iron.

—That's clever, said my little sister Ariane, and if you had blown it? When you want to kill someone you take a gun, not a . . .

That day I said that I didn't have a gun, that first of all I didn't know how to shoot, and that I wouldn't have fucked it up. Then we shook Abel, still stiff and irradiated and busy going gaga on the spot due to a short-circuit that was lasting much longer than usual.

—Pay close attention to Abel, said my mother pushing the door with her knee because her arms were full of laundry and bottles. It's not too bad, he'll come through it.

—I told you so, grumbled my sister Ariane straightening a pleat in her skirt that had twisted. A gun or nothing. That's clever.

Abel finally collapsed and I had just enough time to fling myself into the path of his fall—always backward, luckily it's easy to keep him from cracking his skull on the corner of the bed. Ariane helped me, without saying anything more, lay him down on it. After which we waited.

My father had bled a lot, which had let a fair amount of suspicious fumes out of his head. He told the doctor the same thing as my mother: that he knocked into the frame of an open window when he stood up after unlacing his work boots. You did a real number on yourself, stated the doctor—which made my little sister Ariane shrug her shoulders, but no one was looking at her except me, and anyway she was too little for anyone to take notice of her—You've got a lump like a potato. The next time that you see two windows instead of one, try to avoid going in-between them—it'll spare you some trouble.

When the doctor had left, my father said again that we were little bastards, that he should have drowned us at birth like rabid kittens. Which proved he was still a bit pickled, since when he was sober, he said absolutely nothing.

Abel, who in the meantime had regained consciousness and come back to us, began to cry as always because he didn't want to be a little bastard. Ariane and I, we shut him up. Abel insisted on saying that, as for him, he had done nothing. The flow came out of him everywhere from his eyes from his nose from the corners of his mouth, like a colourless blood of which he was going to empty himself in front of our eyes. But it had been a long time since anyone went crazy for so little, except maybe my mother—the Mothers were almost always occupied with wiping up something, tears drops of wine spilt on the tablecloth pee-soaked diapers slobber on the kids' chins or the soap foam on the tile floors . . . —My mother therefore took out her handkerchief to wipe Abel, knelt halfway down in front of him There there sweetheart there there . . . My father looked at them sideways from underneath his bandages squinting his eyes because of his aching head. In the end he began to holler that no one had done anything, shit! That's understood. And now get the fuck out.

—Go play, said my mother like it was both normal and a death sentence, playing, for kids. Go play then. After having dried Abel off, she wiped up the forgotten little drops of blood on the linoleum. And let your father sleep, be good, for once. You can see that he's hurt.

—Do you want me to tell you, Ariane said to me checking the pleats of her skirt with an imperceptible pinching of her fingers, it's neither here nor there to me.

Abel was still losing a little fluid here and there slowing down.—Sniff, Ariane said showing him how. It's not going to last your whole life, no. Or at least wipe your nose.

I can still hear Ariane saying to me, with a rate of speech like an avalanche where all the words knocked themselves over mixed themselves together and fought among themselves, that it would have been better if Abel 'passed' without making a scene, because sometimes you'd wonder if it was worth the trouble, no but really . . .

I don't remember when I learnt it (you don't pay attention to things like that) but I knew very early, and Ariane too, that one could 'get rid of' kids that had barely been conceived by swallowing some kind of shit. We knew well that, in the first weeks of germination, almost every kid in the street was treated like difficult indigestion. We were all survivors of the great invasion, so ferociously planted in the belly of our mothers that they had to finish us off by will or by force to make us finally let go Race of champions. Or race of traitors, creeping into the corners. Ariane is of the race of champions: it seems that my mother almost died, but not her. But in the end, my mother always told her friends, between raising one more kid or leaving two little orphans, the choice is quickly made . . . Sighing, she had allowed Ariane to grow, she who was already so obstinate.

—You didn't know how to take care of it, Gertrude said to my mother, taking on her cheeky counsellor voice.

—And you? said my mother with a certain annoyance, you knew?

—Me, said Gertrude, they tricked me once but not twice. I was sorry enough the first time to want to learn . . .

Brutal silence in Margot's kitchen where the Mothers twist on their chairs looking like they don't dare let out even a little burp. Finally, they pull it together, focusing on melting a particularly recalcitrant sugar cube in their cups.

—And what's up with this sugar? Micheline finally says tapping on it with her spoon.

—Belgian sugar, says Margot. It's Gaston, he has a pile of it. Real shit, just between us, what's it good for?

—In any case, says my mother, in coffee it's crap.

—It doesn't melt, adds Micheline. And when it melts, it doesn't sweeten . . . Give me another one, here, doll.

—That Gaston, says Gertrude, he always has messed up stuff. It's not so bad, this sugar, stop bitching.

Between us, Margot always said to my mother as soon as Gertrude was gone—and preferably Micheline too, always so hung up on her Principles that one—Between us, Gertrude, what a shitty life she's had, when you think about it . . .

—I know, my mother always said But still.

—Raised like a Prussian, Margot insisted. Strrrrict. Strrrrict. The parents were strict. The curate was strict. A childhood of strict goose-stepping. *Heil! Heil!* said Margot stiffening her double chin to show my mother. Us, we really have no idea what that was like, not really . . .

—No, admitted my mother, it's true, we don't really have any idea . . .

The story, we knew it by heart, but we always listened, because once in a while a detail would be slightly modified.

Gertrude had caught a young one, no one really knew how—maybe even with a stiff uniform without any wrinkles, she had never said—And then afterwards her father took the whip off the hook The mother threw her out in the street The open door the silent treatment It was a big scene of Dishonour while in the street you could hear a regiment of boots tap tap tap on the paving stones . . . It was in 1939, where could she go?

—Ah, I know, said my mother. But . . .

No one knew how Gertrude landed up in France, nor with whom, this wasn't very clear Nor above all how she learnt French, that she speaks like everyone else only tripping a little over her words as if it was just a personal tic, a lack of momentum, a particular type of apathy . . .

—One shouldn't throw stones, admits Micheline whom no one ever hears coming and who erupts sometimes in a conversation when one wasn't expecting her. One can't, surely, it was a foul time. But . . .

She sniffs the snot of her chronic cold, takes out her handkerchief to mop herself up and her knitting to keep her hands busy. But even still . . .

And Margot who cannot change topic like that, it would be too obvious, Margot continues her soap opera, polishes it and sands it down, so well that one knows a little more with each replay. Because having become French by marriage with some unlucky Dupont, Gertrude gave birth at the same time that Hitler was invading Poland. And bam! There was Dupont taken, and sent to the 'Phoney War' where he blew away like smoke, a rough current of air . . . In 1940, Gertrude was on the highway with her baby An ant among the ants The planes with the swastikas fired on them all without distinction Gertrude is afraid of the Germans Gertrude is afraid of the French Gertrude is afraid of everyone.

—Oh, I hear you, sighed my mother hopelessly.

—That poor kid, adds Micheline wiping her dripping nose with every sentence, it's a real hard-luck story, one can't say . . . .

The Mothers grow quiet. They look at their nails their stitches or the floor. Margot reheats the coffee which will boil again because she forgets the time groping around among the cups for some Gauloises. They think about Gertrude. About Gertrude's kid, who's called Mylene Who never plays with the other kids Whom we all see at her window, up there, with her pretty little face always so sad.

It's because she's being punished, says Gertrude brusquely. And my mother lifts her eyes with a jolt As if lifted by a big wave As if she was going to slam completely into Gertrude's impassivity:

—Punished . . . Punished . . . I'd like to know for WHAT you punish her like that all the time, that poor kid!

—Clearly, says Gertrude, you never heard her talk back to her father.

But aside from the fact that her 'father' is not her father, adds Micheline, he's got to be at least the fourth one, what do you expect . . . .

That, of course, they don't say to Gertrude. Not any more, it's useless, Gertrude becomes compact and heavy and silent at the subtlest allusion, and ends by leaving as stiff and rigid as if she were pushed out by the barrel of a gun.

So the Mothers shut up, each one tapping on her sugar cube to make it melt faster, so hard that drops of coffee splattered everywhere and Ariane got indignant with her voice lowered What the hell! If it was us who made up shit like that . . . I automatically corrected: If it were we who were making up. Who were making up, Ariane consented, never mind.

—Oh man, said Gertrude as if it were the natural conclusion of this floating silence that she hadn't identified, you have no idea how much I regretted that time . . .

In the sweetness of that voice lightly muffled and dragging and whose vibrations seemed to linger in the air long after she went silent, I suddenly feel all my mother's nerves tighten scramble themselves tie themselves into a knot.

—Obviously, said my mother tipping over her cup because she was leaning so hard on her sugar cube. Oh shit! Sorry. Obviously . . . It must be a question of spite. Me, I have no regrets. Excuse me, Margot, no no, gimme the sponge, I can't believe how clumsy I am. Me, you see, I never held it against my kids. It's not their fault, the poor kids!

—When they're there, adds Micheline, lifting each of the cups one after another so my mother can wipe up, when they're there you forget everything. It's really true . . . Shit, the coffee! Margot, the coffee.

—Margot goes on a rampage, turning off the gas with one hand under the pot that was reheating and that is overflowing with blackish foam, while lighting from the other burner a mashed cigarette that was saved a little too hastily from the flood.

Gertrude shrugs her shoulders and lets her voice linger, with irony or tenderness, you can't tell:

—But me neither, I don't . . .

—They're so little, fragile. So at the mercy of an accident or an act of thoughtlessness . . . For months you get no sleep, for fear that they forget to breathe at night, that they choke while spitting up . . .

—It's true, it's true, adds Margot who never had a kid but who would have done the same.

—Oh! It's okay, says Gertrude. I've got your number And afterwards they're so cute when they begin to drool to crawl around on all fours, to speak real words . . . You can fill in the rest, you get the picture. Besides, it's time for me to go. 'Night everybody!'

—That Gertrude, says my mother as the door slams, there are times when I wanna knock her block off. Don't you?

—It makes me feel funny, whispers Ariane while Margot stirs the boiled coffee in the pot to bring it back to a decent consistency, it makes me feel funny . . . Like a refugee, doesn't it?

Abel doesn't say anything, as always. It's like he's deaf. He plays jacks.

—Do you want any more of this mud? asks Margot with a measure of conciliation.

—No thanks, says Micheline getting up in turn, it boiled over three times already.

—But, you don't want me to throw it out, though! Margot says indignantly bringing her pot forward resolutely.

—Keep it for your breakfast tomorrow, suggests my mother. At this time of day, I won't drink any more either, it'll ruin my sleep. Let's go kids, on your feet. Camille, I'm talking to you, mark your page and come on.

We kiss Margot whose beard scratches. It smells of smoke, burnt coffee and the chamber pot. But at Margot's, it's like being at home, except at our house there are toilets.

I tell Ariane that it's not a big deal to be refugees, as long as they love us. I say it to her far from my mother who might hear us, but near enough to Abel so that he benefits from it as well. They are little. They don't get how hard it is to live. I feel like I owe them this kindness.

But the next morning, when we were going to get milk, Ariane seemed more worried than usual and had tears at the edges of her lashes.

—What's wrong?

—Nothing. I'm thinking.

I let her think. But a little further along:

—We almost died, do you realize that?

—But we're not dead.

—It doesn't matter, said Ariane sniffling with all her might.

—And why are you sniffling, huh? said Marie-who-has-two-sexes interrupting her raking of the gutter.

—Because, said Ariane, who didn't keep secrets from anyone. I almost died before I was born.

—Ah, said Marie seriously, so you're crying for yourself even as you're living?

Ariane sniffs without responding. Marie-who-has-two-sexes is round and short like a tower, shod in soldier's shoes, wrapped in her blue city-worker shirt. She has a moustache, a bucket and a broom, and a little rubbish cart whose wheels grate. Above the vertical wrinkles that break up her cheeks, her eyes are clear under her grey hair. She has, above all, an enormous voice, which sweeps everything before her, and a matching laugh.

—Oh well, says Marie in her enormous voice which covers you entirely, you're pretty alive from what I can tell. So?

—But we weren't made on purpose! Ariane counters while striking me to keep me from dragging her along.

—Wipe your nose, says Marie-who-has-two-sexes, setting down her broom and taking out her handkerchief that's as big as a dish towel.

—Before being born . . . says Marie whose clear eye goes back and forth between Ariane and me. Hmph! Who didn't almost die before being born? You think you're alone? Look at this.

And she yanks up a dandelion that was growing on the edge of the sidewalk. It's my job to pull that up. So look here, all that, it's nothing but little seeds. Supposing that a little wind . . .

Marie blows on the flower, like the picture in the *Petit Larousse* dictionary. Here, we call them flyers, you see, because they fly all over the place, with their big fuzzy bristles. And look where that falls . . . On the road. In my car. On the roofs. In a chimney. Just anywhere. Do you believe that each seed will become a flower?

—I dunno, says Ariane, wiping her nose with indifference.

—Well, not at all, says Marie. Only one or two will fall in a little piece of land where they can germinate and make another flower, not counting the fact that someone pays me to pull them up. So, you see, they grow anyway, let's say one in a hundred . . . Nature, my little chickadees, it's nothing but an enormous waste. For the seeds of children, it's the same, there are some that get pulled up, and others that grow . . .

She coughs, considers us with disgust, and concludes:

—So, little donkey? You're a little seed who got lucky, and you're crying? You're not content to be here, growing nice and tall, in the sun?

Cut it out, said Marie in her biggest voice while taking up her tools, her broom. And never let me catch you again in such great despair over trivial details. Dum-dum.

All the same, the Mothers, I wonder if they realized   Or if they thought us deaf or dumb or what.

Luckily, the little ones weren't there when they teased Micheline—Gertrude leading the charge, as always—about her last little one, Ogino.

Gertrude was laughing, with her laugh so vast and hollow and so warm that it made you want to drown in it. Ha ha ha! The rhythm method   It's the day   It's not the day   Ha ha ha!

—And anyway, said my mother who didn't notice me any more, it ain't possible, and anyway you think that 'my man', when he wants it, that he's going to care about that, whether it's the right day? You've got to make compromises in your household, if you want peace, my mother used to say.

Compromises. That's what we all were. I shut my book without even marking my page, and I fled like a zebra. I was about the age that Ariane is now, I don't remember exactly.

—But what? yelled Ariane from the toilet. What do you want?

—Get out.

—But I haven't finished! I've barely started . . .

—It doesn't matter, get out. Quiiiick! I'm going to throw up.

Later, we grow up. We become parents, without knowing how: even the Mothers remember having been little. They maintain a sort of astonishment about it, as if they had been moved along by surprise.

But one will not have been able to 'move' Abel. I don't know why. I won't know.

He was handsome, Abel—Too handsome to be true, said my mother in her moments of adoration—And we didn't love him. We didn't love him not because he was handsome (the reverse would have been more logical, a pleasing physique generally exerts a sort of fascination on one's entourage) nor because my mother loved him too much: she loved us all 'too much' and we knew it perfectly well. But Abel was handsome in a strange and suspect way and it hollowed out around him an impalpable zone of emptiness. Abel's was a repulsive beauty, there's no other word for it.

—Will Abel be there? our pals would ask with a grimace whenever we would propose a game or an outing. Ariane and I would always hold firm: Abel would be there. Abel who never knew how to make his own friends Abel who followed us, Ariane or me, or Ariane and me, as if there was nowhere else to go.

We, even Ariane who was the smallest, constantly and efficiently ensure his physical protection, because he is our brother. And also by a vague sense of justice that keeps our conscience clean.

—With us, Abel is safe everywhere in the world. And everywhere in the world he has a void around his body like an imaginary bubble that keeps others at a distance.

Ariane and me never talk about our feelings for Abel. Between us it's a tacit and silent terror, a slab that could sink heavily into the abyss.

And now, as though from the opposite bank, I watch Abel who is growing up. Still as handsome as ever, his eyes bright like two wide open holes in his head shining a light coming from nowhere and going right through you.

When he has his fits, he gets stiff, as though irradiated from within, and he goes pale as a corpse. He topples over all of a sudden, without saying a word, without crying out for help.

It's not epilepsy: he doesn't thrash around, doesn't foam at the mouth. He doesn't throw up either when he comes to. We don't know what it is. We'll never know: the electrodes that they put on his skull didn't detect anything abnormal. In any event, he swallows little white pills that he has to keep on taking, even though they don't have any noticeable effect on him. The doctor says that it's necessary to wait, but for what?

While waiting, my father works, drinks a little, and says nothing. My mother goes to Margot's every afternoon, where she meets her friends from the block in a haze of boiled coffee of Margot's Gauloises of various light tobacco cigarettes of Gertrude's the German who has been French in any case for quite some time. On leaving school, that's where we go to find her. Or else on Thursdays, when it rains.

Margot's chin pricks a bit. She's small and fat, and she has asthma. The oldest, she's about sixty. After her, there's Gertrude who has a moustache almost as black as her mane, but silken, with dark eyes, a voice as velvety as her eyes, and teeth that are still pretty. Broad shoulders, too, located at a respectable height, and a very impressive torso. She spends the morning shift at the factory. In the afternoon, she rejoins the others after a short nap. Micheline and my mother are the youngest. Micheline is thick like a fireplug, with eyes of a fragile, worn out blue that are always drowning in the water of a cold that's getting worse or getting better but that never completely disappears. My mother, she's my mother. She has nothing but singular traits We detect her by her sounds her smell and even the vibrations in the air that let us know immediately of her absence or presence without needing to explore each room in the house. We recognize her in the dark under the rubble under the mud and even very far underground . . .

—And HIM? asks Ariane, solely with the intention of cornering me.

Generally, I shrug my shoulders.

Except for that infamous rock that one must not throw at Gertrude but that makes everyone's hands itch, except for my mother's obstinate refusal to admit that one should perpetually punish a child, and the clearly expressed suspicion that Gertrude above all doesn't dare vex her little Jules—recognized unanimously as a 'real asshole'—, they get along rather well. They talk about their lives. Above all, strangely, of their life before. As if now they were excluded or exiled, in the gloom of the flat years, the years of nothingness.

—You know, says Margot passing her coffee her nose on the filter, the butt of her cigarette wedged sideways and its smoke getting in her eye that starts to run all of a sudden—Oh! shit, I can see less and less—You know that I saw Mimosette again? She stopped in for a drink in passing, the other morning. It's been a dog's age since I ran into her.

—Who? says Micheline whose eyes were also running because of a relapse.

—Mimosette, you know very well who I mean. The one who used to sell cheese with me before the war. Afterwards, she was widowed and she sold mimosa flowers on the sidewalks, that's the one.

—Oh! The big hunchbacked whore, with the purple mug?

—That's it, that's the one. She never could tolerate the cold, the poor old thing . . .

—Yeah . . . She drinks a bit too, sometimes?

—Yes, admits Margot, changing her cig to the other side. Yes, it's true, she drinks.

—And what's she doing, now?

—Hmph! Still the mimosas . . . Some rags, some odds and ends.

—What suffering! sighs my mother who also can't tolerate the cold and who empathizes all the more.

Micheline, as a good Christian, is not far from thinking that this abject poverty is the payment for Sin, what do you expect, all those women who lived the Life . . .

—The Life . . . The Life . . . Margot crabs sniffing her filter with a certain irritation Maybe you think it's easy, the Life? Let's see you go out and work for a living, once in a while?

—Let's not fly off the handle, says Gertrude who finished her paper and refolded it, now now . . . But you were really a holy bunch, don't deny it . . .

Margot doesn't deny it. She keeps pouring boiling water on the coffee grounds with a little smile on her lips drawing back over her missing teeth. Even though there was a sort of haze floating over her past, or imagined, exploits, one could see that even still she had no remorse.

—There was Renée, said Gertrude as though she had been part of the troop, you remember? With her limp hair . . .

—Yes, says Margot suddenly opening up. She was going blind drunk on milk and kirsch, let me tell you. Who would have believed that? To the waiter, she always used to say 'Gimme the usual', and he brought her a glass of milk. She looked like a real angel in the midst of us with our big glasses of Beaujolais. And at the end of the day, without anyone seeing her drink anything except milk, she was half-baked . . . Really weird. It all came out when the neighbourhood bistro closed down. Crazy Renée!

—And who else was there? asked Ariane who was fascinated by the former friends of Margot as if they were characters from legends.

Well, there was Mimosette, yes, two or three others whose names Margot forgot since it was so long ago, sometimes Marie-who-has-two-sexes . . .

—But really, is it true or not, that she has two sexes?

—I haven't seen for myself, says Margot putting down the empty pot. They say she does.

—It's possible, says Gertrude adding to the general uncertainty. It happens.

—All I know, is that she made deliveries for a clothing designer, to the homes of very chic people. Back in the day, she had been an artist . . .

—What kind of artist? asks my mother, painter, actress, or what?

Nobody really knew. Marie, she was never much of a talker, except with kids. And then, no one ever asked her questions, it wasn't done. Besides, she didn't like that, questions. She was content to laugh at them loud enough to cause the glasses on the counter to clatter without ever answering except with jokes. What a voice she has, that Marie. Like she's just popped her cork.

—Even still . . . says my mother who is impressed by the Arts. And now there she is scraping the gutter . . . What a life!

—There are highs and lows, sighs Gertrude with her voice lagging as though it were the moral of every story.

—And then, says Micheline hugging her knees to her chest, it's an odd setting, you can't deny it. No advance warning or anything. 'They' gorge themselves on everything, and then they find themselves on the street.

Marie-who-has-two-sexes found herself on the street. With a broom with stiff bristles to clean the gutters, a little cart to gather the trash, and two little red calves between her coat and the socks rolled down over her work shoes. She never said very much. She pulls up the dandelions to make things nice, and never laughs any more.

Margot doesn't know if Marie had much to 'feast on' or if that went back to Methuselah, and if she ever had any money, she would have been right to enjoy it, what would she do with it now? Treat her rheumatism? Not worth it, there's no cure.

There were also some fishmongers who feared nothing. And above all, there was Aimée from Marseille, who was actually from Brittany, and who disappeared so mysteriously during the war.

My mother remembered, with that strange astonishment of a child displaced all of a sudden. She was a young girl. She liked her, Aimée from Marseille, with her accent. We would buy fish from her twice a week when she went by with her cart. In our day that isn't really done any more, but it was practical . . . What became of her, Aimée? Maybe she died?

—Oh, surely, says Margot, riffling through the sideboard looking for cups, otherwise, we would have seen her again. How is it possible that there's one missing? I know I had six . . .

—There are only four of us, says Gertrude, why are you making yourself crazy? You'll find it.

Nothing's where it belongs, says Margot with a sudden despondency, everything's up in the air in this stinking world.

The Mothers should have killed themselves   Or let themselves die   It was the only logical step in the situation. But no. Very few died, of those among them. They had a stubborn resistance, animal-like   The passive resistance of things half buried. The men climbed on top of them, knocked them about sometimes, weighed on their conscience as much as on the rhythm of their days   The kids screamed vomited grew fell sick escaped went bad . . . The Mothers endured it all   The knocking down of days one after another endlessly   The eternal circuit house-shops-girlfriends and repeat   The persecution of trifling things The grumblings chores bullying Running for cash to the neighbours who might still have some while waiting for payday or the government cheque ... When everything got too bad, they all made noise about their feeble hope for a miracle: the 'grown son' who might find work, the little one who might not catch chickenpox this week now is not the time despite the epidemic, the lottery ticket that might just win, for crying out loud, for once. They had sudden moments of madness Whims fits of laughter.

Then my mother would come back, as if she were drunk, with a mischievous gleam in her eye. She dared to bring up Australia, and kangaroos to my dad ... Shit, said my father, snapping his newspaper Stop it with your bullshit Give me something to eat, I've been waiting for an hour. She served him, as though it were her duty, but without any particular respect A man so pig-headed Immobile Nailed to the putrefied parquet like a plant in its pot Why did she have to end up with him. That man there, stupidly determined to die in the exact spot where he had come out of his mother's belly ... While in Australia ... The sound of the rustling newspaper covered my mother's voice which kept on going, for our ears only. After the war, it's true, right, they could have emigrated Made their fortune Changed their life ... We knew almost everything about Australia, in the end: the kangaroos the rabbits the dingoes ...

—You're the dingo, my father cut in. You speak English?

—We would have learned it, my mother maintained in a voice a little sobered all the same. We would have gotten by . . . .

Only the sound of the mangled newspaper answered her. My mother faded away entirely in the end. We knew well that Germany had forever turned my father off the idea of expatriation, fixing in his heart the unbreakable resolution to kick the bucket at home in France rather than anywhere else on the globe. In her normal state, my mother understood that. But after a fit of crazy laughter, an end of the month crisis, a crisis about the future, she became idiotic and infantile again and would go on harping about her nostalgia for kangaroos.

Though I might go on from time to time about Australia, just to annoy my father, the little ones would stick to the America from the Westerns that we could see at the movies. Ariane wouldn't go out any more without her lasso, which she used adroitly to tame fountains and signposts. Me too, said Abel, I'm going to America. With you. We're all going to Ameeeerica, cried Ariane with her arms outspread and her face to the grey sky It's an awesome country with canyons and horses, yippeeee!

One morning when Ariane was shouting like that about the Americas, her arms flung towards a tepid little sun which was yellowing the edges of the clouds, Marie-who-has-two-sexes stopped scraping her gutter to smile at us. She had horse teeth, pretty grey eyes, the wind in her hair which stood up on her head, her boobs on her belly as usual, and little white socks rolled over her ankle boots.

—Hello, said Ariane. Is it true, or not, that you have both sexes?

And we were almost bowled over by the gigantic burst of laughter from Marie that exploded over our heads:

—Who is it who told you that load of crap, my little 'chickadee'?

It's true her voice sounded as though it came out of a barrel after it had been banged around at length on the floorboards. Just in case, Ariane grabbed onto my belt, and I could feel Abel trembling behind my back. I said that Ariane didn't know, that she was too little, that she must excuse her . . . While wiping her tears of laughter with her immense checked handkerchief, Marie, then, asked me:

—And you, you know?

When I didn't find anything to say in response, Marie, sticking her handkerchief in the pocket of her blouse, grumbled that it didn't matter, that one day I would know everything, and I would explain it to her, to Ariane and to that other one, there, who was about to climb under my shirt. And in the meantime we should shut our ears to busybodies' dirty stories, bah!

On that note she began to scrub her gutter with gusto, in the sun that had not made up its mind to shine.

—And what are you up to there? said my mother bringing in the garbage, instead of going to do the errands. Have you seen the time? What is your father going to eat? Haven't you finished loafing about?

Kids are always accused of 'loafing about'. Above all in summer, because of vacation. It's suddenly as though they had nowhere to put us. They had to clear us off the narrow path where the big people are going forward and all know where they are going. Us, we're planted there We're in the way They send us on missions, and get on it, or else they take us and make us walk straight on the path held on a tight leash to make it through the day.

—I've had enough of seeing you hangin' around, said my father who sometimes was restored to speech by one little drink too many. C'mere, I'm going to teach you how to play petanque. And he dragged me, like it was a punishment, to the last empty lot in the neighbourhood. Ariane was allowed to follow on our heels as a mere spectator.

My father never played with us, or with anyone else. It's a bear, my mother always said. And the provenance of those petanque balls, which I never saw again, remains such a mystery to me while I lean on a perfectly clean window pane that separates me from the empty street, completely empty except for the leaves whose sound I invent—I truly believe I invent, because how else would I hear it—the sound of a very light crushing.In fact this is, muffled to the level of a murmur and seemingly anaesthetized, the sound of reeds that I have in my head   And in order to keep myself from being contaminated by that sound, I invent other ones, which don't bite or which bite very little on the numb memory. And I place my burning hands on the window, to numb them too in this cold that empties the brain and the heart to the point where one imagines oneself on the verge of dissolving, like a little condensation on the glass.

Clara would also look out on the street, through her windowpane. It was here, or not far, but still so far away. I approach, as though a cord pulls me   Like each time that I perceive her or glimpse her or imagine recognizing her. She smiles at me, gestures towards the lock   But I make a sign to her: No no she shouldn't open Not worth it It's so cold this Winter. From one side and the other side of the pane, we watch each other in silence in a time abruptly fallen behind, independent of watches, without any parameters.

Then I place my hand, fingers spread, on the cold of the glass. She has a sort of very slow hesitation, during which her gaze is in mine, feeling it, examining it . . . Then, as though invincibly attracted, her hand comes to put itself exactly on top of mine, on the other side of the glass. I believe I can perceive the warmth, the imperceptible pulsing of blood. I lean a little harder, barely. And immediately there is nothing under my fingers, under my palm, but this surface infinitely smooth and frozen and hard as metal. I feel cold in my wrist like someone had just cut it.

I leave quickly, in my pocket that disappeared hand—cut neatly off—which has no longer any weight or shape.

I distance myself from the window as though I had just burnt myself on it. Is there no longer any neutral surface, the smallest space where one can relax without always running into oneself, reflecting one's own image to infinity as in a prison of mirrors . . . Think about anything, the Mothers and their stories, petanque and what followed, why not. Stay calm and forget who I am, if I ever knew it, and anyway how would I have known it except by process of elimination by trying out everything that I'm not but what a hassle and why bother in the end . . . I've noticed that I've always been relatively immobile—except when I was killing my father—as though avoiding the breaking the shattering of things around me, the disaggregation of this minuscule universe where I seemed to grow too strong. I wonder who you look like, my mother often said, innocently highlighting the awareness that I already had of being a dangerous substance because I was strange.

Really I do wonder . . . In order to put to rest these suspicions—my own above all—I remain as still as a tree, and they temporarily forget about me. Then my father comes upon me, spots me by my traitorous mug, and spars with me to assimilate me into the ranks: after all I am HIS child. There must be some little connection, even a craggy or tortuous path, a possible access route . . . C'mere I'm going to teach you to play petanque. But of course I don't understand it. He bugs me. Moving bugs me. Everything bugs me at that time, except grammar rules that we learn at school, where I feel like an intelligent rat in a maze, and the printed page that swallows you up in the same way, without making a scene, without alerting anyone.

I lived my childhood as if under anaesthesia with the grey sky above my head and inside things moving like smoke. For a long time, it left me with a certain incapacity to distinguish the real from the imaginary A way of living mounted upon a poorly defined boundary, neither all the way in nor all the way out And the fixed obsession with getting myself knocked over once and for all on the wrong side, I didn't know which one, where you would stay stuck in perpetuity, definitively outside of everything as only those who wall themselves off can be. All that remains is the reflex to flee, and as a result with this concession: okay, I obey my father Or at least I try Or at least I pretend to.

But a petanque ball is heavy. That one is deeply grooved, doubtless to keep it from slipping, but in fact it doesn't slip and it rips off the skin of one's fingers. Throw! says my father, like this. And he shows me for the hundredth time how to do it, the arm hanging, the hand wrapped around the ball, supple, the trunk arched, legs together and knees bent. Supple. Supple. Like elastic. Go on, throw it!

My father is in front of the setting sun Right in front One would say that the rays shine out from his body Supple supple legs together and knees bent the arm swings with the hand at the end hanging half closed on the ball, he shows me again Go on, throw it! In the end he stays squatting, watching the target ball that he is pointing out to me with his finger because now the sun is in my eyes He has been bugging me with this crap for an eternity because he has nothing to do today, because he's hungover, and because Ariane is too little, she can barely lift these dirty balls. I don't give a shit, about his bullshit about staying supple and bent   My hands hurt   I'm going to throw this thing that's burning me, and as far away as possible   And this time will be the last time, even if he gives me a good thrashing   My stiffened arm swings like a catapult, and the ball flies as if shot from a canon, straight into the sun.

—Not like . . . Ah!

He sprang up, passed again in front of the sun then below it. He must have been laid flat his entire length: the grass had swallowed him whole. Since he wasn't moving nor shouting nor anything, I finally approached.

He was hit by the ball right between the eyes. He was, as one says, pushing up daisies. Dropped dead.

—What do you mean 'dropped dead'? Ariane, whom I had finally found in a ditch where she had gone off to take a piss I don't know how long ago, was asking me, did you really kill him?

She was pulling on the elastic of her panties as if she wanted to draw them up to her neck. Are you shitting me?

—See for yourself.

She came. She saw. You couldn't say it was a pretty sight. We're going to get totally balled out, said Ariane, and on top of that it's late: the sun's gone down.

Then my father started hollering, both hands first on the hole but then also on his eyes because it must have hurt too much and with the blood he couldn't see anything any more But what are you waiting for, you bunch of idiots, go get your mother or someone, eh? You want me to die? And he rolled around on the ground with his hands waving about, not knowing where to put them any more. Camille . . . Camille go get your mother. Right now, you hear me?

Since he was trying to get up, we ran straight to the house. If you want my opinion, Ariane was saying, he wasn't dead enough. We should have stayed a little longer in the ditch . . .

Now, Ariane was saying even as she was following me at a good clip, we have to go get help. Too bad.

Afterwards my father said that we weren't children but wolves, or something like that. Budding assassins. And it would have been better to kill us before we grew up.

Even though the attacks invariably came from me, my father always refused to disassociate me from the others—Little shits You really are little assholes I ask you . . . —to attribute individual responsibility to me, to leave out the others who obviously had done nothing. As if he knew for all eternity that Ariane was with me. Or as if he didn't want to see that Abel would never be with anyone.

But now who is with me? And even where am I exactly? I would like to go back to Margot's To have never stopped being at Margot's house, there where we attained the highest level of invisibility The little ones playing in the corner, practically under the chairs Me reading Ariane pulling me by the sleeve, whispering her questions in my ear, getting fed up with it all and asking to go for a walk . . . Abel never asking for anything We didn't know if he was listening In any case he was watching, with his big eyes bright and staring. It was yesterday. It's today. The mothers are chatting. We barely exist, muted, protected from surveillance by the fact of our proximity. We're good. Peaceful. We're bored, or else we listen:

—The last time that I saw her, Aimée from Marseille, Margot was saying, ooh la la if I had known, it was during the exodus. They were refusing to take her cart on board the Honfleur ferry They were only taking people at that point, with their baggage, because they were being fired on, it wasn't the time to hang around . . .

Oh! What a bunch of wimps, she was yelling, Aimée, where was the French army, those guys are going to cut us up like sausage! Lousy Führer! Stinking planes! So there are no more soldiers in this country. Holy Mother! To shoot at women and children . . . Bullshit! Torturers!

While they were trying to detach Aimée from the cart that she was clinging to while screaming, the ferry left without us and it was blown to smithereens in the middle of the Seine. Aimée abruptly shut up, as if someone had smacked her. We took the road to Rouen, in the hope that the bridges were still standing And in the enormous crowd that stopped the cart from advancing, we lost Aimée from Marseille who had maybe already stopped somewhere in another fit of rage . . . Oh, if we had known . . .

Margot filled the cups while sniffling, because that Aimée, she was somebody. In Marseille, she was on the map—What's that mean, to be on the map? whispered Ariane to me—Shhh! Shit—and then one fine day she had enough and she pulled out. As far away as possible, to escape her pimp who would have strung her up like Christmas lights if he had found her. Besides, maybe it is for the best, gosh, what happened . . .

—No, no, says Gertrude, don't sweat it, he surely had other fish to fry at that time.

Even still, she was a pistol, Aimée from Marseille. Oh how we laughed in those days And anyway the guy that she had chosen for herself he was not the best, I tell you . . . Oh! An honest guy, a fisherman But then . . . It's really simple, the minute he sobered up, he fell under the wheels of a truck, it just wasn't his normal state. A good-looking corpse at least, rest in peace. You should have seen the beatings that she got, Aimée. And for no reason at all. Oh! Sonofabitch, she would say Oh! Holy Mother, I thought he was going to tear my limbs off!

—Sonofabitch? repeats Ariane, really low, elbowing me so that I would translate.

—I don't know. It's slang from Marseille.

But Aimée had more than one trick up her messed-up sleeve. She knew all the cops from her working days, and among them there were some good guys, otherwise nice and friendly like she was, and not looking at the weight of the merchandise, cop or not, they would have bent over backwards for her.

Come, she would say to one of the cops on the beat, I'll pay you for a job. Listen, could you do me a favour? My dick of a husband is in the bistro next door. Completely wasted, let me tell you. Will you lock him up for me, huh? It'll give me a night's peace. I haven't slept for three days I've got bruises in places I'm too embarrassed to show you And me, I work, you see me, I'm no streetwalker. So how 'bout it, you're a good guy, will you keep him in jail as long as the law allows, on whatever charge you can come up with?

Jeannot the fisherman spent the night in lockup, and the next day it started over again . . .

—And why didn't she leave him? asks Ariane, since she had already done it once?

The Mothers jump in their seats, notice our existence, raise their eyebrows.

—Oh, Margot says scraping the bottom of her cup where the sugar is glued, it's just not that easy . . . You can't spend your whole life running away from everything Have to find another job Have to make new friends . . . to say nothing about the fact that men are the same everywhere, more or less. What do you want, that's life . . .

—There are ups and downs, Gertrude confirms lighting one of her caramel-scented cigarettes, gotta get that into your head.

Yeah. But me, Ariane would always say to me when we would go out for some air, I won't keep a man who boozes, you can count on it. Nor who slaps me around, they're sick. Even if I have to move a hundred times, Ariane would say, I'll fucking get out, until I find one who doesn't drink. Even if I have to go to

America to find him. Don't you agree? And Ariane, who needs to move begins to prance about singing at the top of her lungs:

'The lovers from Havre[2]
Don't need the sea
And the boats are so sad
Being always at sea

'I love you you love me we love each other
Until the end of the world
Because the world is round
My love, don't worry
My love, don't worry'

She has a robust voice, sharp, slightly metallic, which carries for remarkable distances. Marie-who-has-two-sexes maintains that she can hear her from four or five streets away. And when by chance she hasn't heard her for several days, she asks me: What's wrong with her, the future Piaf? Sore throat?

Ariane has a toothache. Or rather, she has a loose tooth and it's bothering her. She never stops wiggling it. My mother says it'll fall out on its own, while you're eating, like the last time, Ariane doesn't have to worry about it. And if I swallow it? Ariane retorts. My mother says, shrugging her shoulder that

2 'Les Amoureux du Havre' by Eddie Constantine.

it won't plug her butthole, and she brings the tray for Abel who is sick.

Ariane carefully avoids any contact between her tooth and food, eating only on one side, moaning every five minutes It's wiggling! It hurts!

Listen, my mother finally says, I'm going to take you to the dentist.—No! yells Ariane clinging to her tooth, it hurts less now than before.

—Then go have it pulled out by Margot, she knows how.

—Oh, no! begs Ariane again, not Margot. I'll take care of it all by myself.

—Then shut the hell up, says my mother. Tie a string to it and pull. Doing it yourself hurts less.

Ariane strung up her tooth with catgut whose reputation for strength was well known. Fifty times that morning she made a go at it. Then at the last minute, her hand would waver, her fingers let the string go at the tiniest pull, the afflicted tooth answered with twinges, the cheek swelled up.

—Today, decides my mother, the dentist is closed, you're lucky. But if it still hasn't fallen out tomorrow, I'm taking you there before you know what hits you.

—No! brays Ariane, I'll get it out.

—Pathetic! Ariane says to me when I refuse yet again to pull on her string.

—Pathetic yourself. You just have to attach it to a door and wait for someone to open it. It's really very simple.

Ariane attaches the end of the string to the door handle, and waits for my mother to enter the room, eyes shut with fear, her hands clutching her own shoulders. When I notice it, I don't have time to warn her: she already had the door banging into her nose, and the tooth was still planted in its aching socket.

—Silly goose, my mother says putting mercurochrome on Ariane's nose, you're supposed to be on the other side of the door, you don't get it.

—You pull on it! yells Ariane who is now suffering in two places on her body. I never saw such chickens as you!

—That's right, says my mother, we're all chickens. Give us a break. Wait for your father. Brave girl, go on!

—No, Ariane says, not him. I'll take care of it by myself if it's gonna be like that.

Now, she has attached her tooth to another string, much longer, that drags on the ground. She hopes to step on it by accident, so that the tooth will fly out in a fit of pain and relief.

This string that she has been dragging around since late morning makes her drool, it gets completely gummy with saliva, sticks to her chin so repugnantly that her pals turn away one after the other with evermore disgusted looks. Ariane becomes furious. Even more so because she can't forget it for even a minute, she's moving about minding her steps crab-like, in order to not step on it. Covered in spit at one end, all dusty on the other, the string becomes an object of general obsession.

Since Ariane, today, was avoiding Margot like the plague, we were hanging out in the street. It's true that Margot pulls her friends' teeth with a pair of common pliers passed through the flame of a lighter beforehand. In Ariane's shoes, I also would've thought twice, even if Gertrude confirms that it was done like that in the Middle Ages, with 'Lout Museek', to distract the patient. In line with this she makes some noise banging two aluminium pot covers together, while she sings—rather brays—in a perfectly imitated drunken voice:

'To drink to drink to dr-i-n-k
We are not leaving without drin-king
No the Normans aren't so crazy
As to leave withouuuuut drinkin'!'

Micheline maintains in vain that she absolutely didn't feel anything, she was so distracted by her joking around, but us we weren't convinced.

First we had to get Abel out of there pronto; the noise, the blood, and the quiet squeaking of the pliers had him on the edge of a meltdown.

Those ladies are crazy, Ariane kept repeating all through our childhood. Crazy. Certifiably crazy.

Call Ariane. But the line is still busy. Call Clara then? No. Clara belongs to another galaxy. And if I thought I could sneak into her space, she would never know how to slip into mine even a little without dying of asphyxia. There was never any possible reciprocity. That, at least, I always knew. Maybe that's why the Mothers are crazy: they have only one world, air tight and very small, where they are locked up without hope of visitors. Without hope of getting out either, except through a hole in the cemetery. How can you blame them for their insanity?

The day this whole business with Micheline's tooth began started with a real three-ring circus, with the laying out of tools all of which were more or less chipped, tarnished, filthy, unusable. Margot was hanging some sconces, one on either side of her side-board. She had seen that in a magazine, it was really sharp. Except that it was on either side of a bed, what a waste of such luxury in a room where you're only going to sleep.

Between Margot's pursed lips, an electrical wire was hanging, stripped at one end. Margot was stripping the other end with a pocket-knife against her thumb.

—What's he up to, that Gaston? Micheline had sighed holding her cheek. This ain't no job for a woman! Oh, Margot says spitting out her wire, don't get me started about him, I'm begging you . . . She twists the little metallic barbs to make them hold together, sticks them in the holes and screws them in, still using the pocket-knife because the screwdrivers all laid out there weren't the right size Doesn't know how to do shit Except his shitty garden His shitty radishes . . .

The sconces are now in place. They're shaky, but nothing could be done about that, no matter how much Margot screws and screws with her pocket-knife. But good enough, right! After all, they ain't coat racks . . .

The Mothers go on mournfully about that Gaston who never does anything right with his own ten fingers (which are only seven anyways, he's cut so many of them off on days when he's so loaded that he hopes to thus gain disability benefits) Poor Margot, she didn't pick a winner with that lazy good-for-nothing-but-emptying-the-neighbourhood-privies-into-his-garden Where nothing grows, on top of that, except wallflowers that smell like shit, and radishes that taste of it.

The lightbulbs, finally screwed into the sconces gave pitiful light. It's like a wake in here! Gertrude declares. Why are the filaments all red? Are you sure it's the right voltage? Margot says yes, that Gertrude can check, besides she's not an idiot. But these lightbulbs are surely for shit, she bought them at the Familistère co-op.

Micheline, her hand still on her cheek, asks if anyone has time to take care of her tooth. Margot says yes, gimme a minute, lemme tidy up this mess, it's not sterile. And to me:

—While you're waiting, Camille, run and get me forty-watt lightbulbs at the drugstore, he's an honest shopkeeper who never sells crap like the department stores forty-watt, you got that?

I come back at a run with the lightbulbs, and Margot changes them, gasping with the beginning of an asthma attack in between puffs of her Gauloise.

—Heh! Gertrude says, it still ain't Versailles. You must have gotten it wrong somewhere in the connections, that ain't right . . .

Margot crushes her cigarette butt with feeling and says to her knowledge there aren't thirty-six ways to connect the wires. It works or it doesn't work, but as for working half-way . . .

—That's the butter dish, says Gertrude.

—What?

—Your butt. You put it out in the frickin' butter dish.

—I don't even know what I'm doing any more, Margot acknowledges separating the ashes from the butter I've got too many things on my mind, that's what it is.

—It looks like there's a loss of power somewhere, maintains Gertrude who is sometimes a little annoying with her technical knowledge.

She suspiciously inspects the new switches that Margot just nailed up:

—You must have messed up the layout of the wires, if you ask me, and the electrical current is divided in two. Because it's really bizarre, we could see better in here with one sixty-watt bulb than with two forties . . .

—It's indirect lighting, Margot cuts in, seemingly trying to convince herself. It's more subtle. Do you want some java?

—What about my tooth? Micheline reminds everyone timidly.

—Oh! Yeah, I ain't got four hands.

—But how come, Micheline complains cradling her cheek, how come the filaments are red?

—Oh! Stop busting my hump, Margot says, with your filaments. You, go get me some coffee before I deal with your tooth. Stork brand, there are little animals in the box, they're for Ariane's collection. I didn't have time to pick some up. What do you want, kids? Some chocolate?

—And some milk, Micheline, Margot yelled through the window.

She says that it's unbelievable, there's always something that needs buying in this house, fucking shit, you can't think of everything . . .

Ariane says that all the same you can't see anything in here. Cut it out, Margot says, or I'll throw everybody the hell out. It's indirect lighting, you can make do just fine.

My mother knocks and comes in and says Oh! . . .

—Oh! . . . what? says Margot who was foraging in the sideboard for something else that was missing now, and spreading ashes everywhere from a new Gauloise.

—Nothing, says my mother hugging Gertrude then Margot who had come out of the sideboard as red as an apple, there's no reason to get yourself in a huff. It's just that you'd think you were in a morgue, with your lamps.

—It's indirect lighting, reassures Gertrude whose light-tobacco cigarette wafts a smell of caramel over the whole mess. But what is she still looking for?

—Sugar, Margot says with a dirty look towards her sconces. I can't find it. What do you expect me to do if the only ones for sale are these half-dead lightbulbs.

My mother prudently concludes that we'll probably get used to it. If Margot wants, she can lend her a bag of sugar. Margot huffs and puffs and sucks in the smoke and says that she'd appreciate it, especially since she just sent Micheline to buy some coffee and some milk with that aching tooth of hers. My mother gives me the keys. In the cupboard on the left. And while you're there take out the trash, at least that will be taken care of. And if your dad is there, tell him that we'll be home soon.

—It's only five thirty, Margot objects.

My mother says yes, but with all these interruptions you never know And then you know how he is . . . And to me, as if there was a risk of a fire or a flood: hurry up!

I shut the door on Gertrude's sighing voice trailing off with unaccustomed sweetness all these men only good for getting on your nerves getting in the way never being there when they're needed but instead always around when they're not . . . The Mothers endure men like a stabbing pathetic pain that you have to get used to, because there is no hope of a cure.

I come back with the sugar at the same time as Micheline with the coffee that she immediately starts to grind. Then Margot passes it around, her nose right up to the filter because it's really true that you can't see a thing with these weak, little lights shit shit shit.

Holding her cheek Micheline says that it makes it cozier They remind her of something these reddish lamps And they all burst out laughing, except Margot who's snuffling at her filter, all the wrinkles in her face pulled together around the butt of her cigarette whose smoke is going right in her eyes.

Afterwards, Margot sterilized the pliers with her lighter, Gertrude howling 'Give us a drink give us a drink give us a drinnnk . . .' while banging her pots, and Ariane and me we dragged Abel out, while the Mothers were beginning the anguished chapter of What-are-we-going-to-make-for-dinner-tonight . . .

I recite from memory for Abel and Ariane: What can I make to eat tonight, do you have any ideas, girls?

—I've had it up to here, Ariane says, of always thinking about the midday meal about the evening meal about the next day's meal Enough already!

—Crepes, suggests Abel who escaped the worst of it and who is coming back to life, or maybe some cooked chocolate.

—Shut up, brats, we're talking seriously here. Me, I always have some packets of soup and some deli meats, and if he isn't happy . . .

—But 'my man' Ariane says sniffling discreetly like Micheline, there's no putting that in front of him. He's a difficult one! And first of all you know he doesn't eat pork.

I say Oh! That's true, with his religion . . .

—His religion, my ass, Ariane says darkly He's never set foot in a mosque, with or without his shoes. It's just to bug me.

Abel objects that he doesn't drink, there's at least that.

—That's all I need for him to drink! Ariane is outraged. No but, you don't think he's enough of a pig as he is?

After that, we quit playing around. We make a flan, Ariane breaking the eggs, me kneading the dough, Abel buttering the dish. At least that'll be worth something, and besides it's what we'd rather eat anyway.

So nothing to do, Ariane says to me kicking a pebble, I won't go to Margot's house, there's nothing to do there. I'd rather have the dentist.

Mylene, Gertrude's daughter, is still at her window bored senseless. Ariane throws her her lasso, at the end of which we have attached the usual basket. The basket overflows with little gifts sent to console

Mylene for her constant isolation: sticks of chewing gum a little bent, caramels as good as new, coloured pencils that aren't too worn out, comics that have seen better days, as well as Ariane's most beautiful marbles because she is happily generous, the animals that come in the coffee that she has doubles of, poems from me wrapped around a bar of chocolate, a pocket knife that Abel found, and whose chipped blades still cut . . . .

Mylene pulls the basket back up at the end of the lasso and asks What is she eating, Ariane, is it string? Our noses in the air, we watch the basket go up. Someone says that girls who are like that at their window, they are daughters of Kings. Mylene says it's really possible, but she doesn't know her father the King. Boys say that the King's daughter always chooses a suitor So Mylene should choose then. And they're all there, their noses in the air, each one surer than the next that he'll be the happy chosen one. I say that to be chosen, you have to have a flower in your hand, and that they don't have anything at all in their dirty, greasy mitts. Anyways, nothing that resembles a flower.

Mylene says okay, she'll choose the one who brings her back the prettiest flower. You have three quarters of an hour. After that, my mom's boyfriend will be back. The boys pretend to throw their hats in the air and scatter like meteors to scour the empty lots, after Mylene specified But a really pretty flower, right? Not a poppy or a buttercup or those shitty wallflowers that Gaston has, I don't want any of those!

—Me, says Ariane whose tongue is caught up in the string, I know where there are zome, zome really pretty vlowers. Zom like she haz never zeen in her live. You want me to tell you where?

—Go on, say it!

—In the dentist's waiting room, says Ariane who is now holding the string so she can speak correctly. If I go there tomorrow, if my tooth hasn't fallen out, I'll steal you one. Surely it'll be the prettiest.

—Tomorrow, will be a little late, my little lady, it's right now that I need it.

—So pull on my string.

—Then we'll never get the flower, neither today nor tomorrow, you nitwit.

Ariane reflects, the string dangling.

After which, she carefully rolls up her lasso:

—Fine. Come with me to the dentist.

—It's closed. He isn't there.

—But his wife is surely there, says Ariane. Wives are always there. We can try.

—But he's the dentist, not her . . .

—Don't worry, says Ariane. It's no magic trick to pull on a string, even you could do it if you didn't have the willies. Good for nothing! I've had enough of this string. And you need a flower. So who cares?

Following on Ariane's heels, I feebly argued a little more:

—But suppose that she says yes, do you have some money to pay her?

—But she doesn't have the right, says Ariane, you just said it: she's not the dentist. You want it, this flower, or don't you want it?

—Are you at least sure that it's pretty?

—Splendid, says Ariane running, the string prudently put away in her pocket. You never saw any like these. I swear.

—But you, says Ariane, braking so sharply that I run into her, you have to swear to me that you'll pull out my next tooth.

—No way, no!

—If you don't swear, says my little sister Ariane, her forehead leaning forward like a goat, I won't go. And without me, your flower is out of reach, I'm the one with the tooth. So do you swear?

The dentist's wife didn't open until the fourth ring of the bell, just as we were getting completely discouraged. She says that her husband is out, that . . .

—I know, I know, says Ariane holding onto her string again in order to speak correctly, but it's today that I hurt.

—She has a tooth that's loose, ma'am, she would like . . .

—It really hurts, insists Ariane, look: it's swelling. Couldn't you pull on it?

The dentist's wife has deep black eyes, soft and motionless, and when she laughs, two dimples on either side of her mouth. It gives us the courage to insist:

—Please, ma'am, she's really in pain . . .

Ariane advances decisively, and the dentist's wife mechanically steps aside to let her pass. I follow them into the waiting room, while the dentist's wife still tries to argue, but with such sweetness and embarrassment and smiling indecision that Ariane registers her protests as so many pleasantries, and expands:

—Ah! I knew it . . . It's nothing at all to pull on it. But me, I don't have the guts. My mother is scared. Everybody's scared. But not you, no, not with your husband's profession . . .

On the side table in the waiting room, there were in fact magnificent flowers in a vase. I'll have to remember to ask Ariane how she knew that: her sources are always shady but reliable.

—Look, Ariane insists, it's swelling.

—It's true, admits the dentist's wife who is bowled over by Ariane's rapid-fire delivery like everyone else and who blinks in the face of it. But just so, if there is an infection . . .

—There's nothing at all, protests Ariane as if one suspected her of dragging in a sleazy sickness, it's a baby tooth. It's just from wiggling it . . .

The dentist's wife sighs, contemplates Ariane with her string and her lasso, and in the end laughs frankly:

—You're a funny duck, with your string. Did your mama send you?

—Yeah right, says Ariane. Mom wanted to wait until tomorrow. But me I've had enough of this string. I wanted to walk on it then have it pop out, but I couldn't do it. I've had it since this morning. This can't go on . . .

And that? asks the dentist's wife putting her finger on the end of her skinned nose.

—I tried with a door, says Ariane with a dark look in my direction, but my mother came in the wrong way.

The dentist's wife laughs a lot. She has eyes that are very black and very pretty, under her gaze you feel like someone really fantastic, but we're not really getting anywhere.

—You're a very determined little girl, the dentist's wife finally says to Ariane. What's your name?

And then, she says with a special effort to keep her tone serious, your name is Ariane . . . You know who Ariane was?

—A car, says my little sister with a peevish air. It's supposed to be a pretty car. My father, when he's loaded, he tells everyone that he has a brand-new Ariane. Me I don't find that funny.

—Me neither, says the dentist's wife whose black eyes become pensive. All right, come on, I'll take care of that tooth. We're going to disinfect it and put a tiny little bit of numbing agent. You won't feel a thing, you'll see.

And to me, still watching me with her beautiful, dark eyes as though I was someone important:

—You don't mind waiting here for two minutes?

—I win, Ariane says foisting her bag of marbles off on me.

—What did you win?

—I had bet that you would agree. Camille never believes anything.

—Camille's wrong, says the dentist's wife staring at me with an extraordinary attentiveness. That's a pretty name too, Camille. You play marbles?

—Yes, says Ariane.

—And you win?

—Easy peasy, says Ariane as the door shuts between them and me.

From Ariane's marble bag, I quickly extract the penknife that's in there with a bunch of random objects that 'might come in handy': minuscule hanks of string, rubber washers, matches and I skip the rest . . . And I cut a flower—the prettiest one—as quickly as possible and at the lip of the vase so it won't be so noticeable.

But the flowers are fake, treachery! All the same, I stuff the cut flower quickly into the marble bag with the penknife and all the other crap, because I don't have time to try to put it back among the others.

—It didn't hurt at all, says Ariane in a clear, loud voice before the door reopens. Thanks a lot, ma'am, I will tell my mother to come by to pay you tomorrow.

—Absolutely not, says the dentist's wife with that almost irrepressible smile that made us believe that we were a perpetual source of satisfaction to her, because I practically didn't do anything . . . And then I'm not a dentist . . . Okay?

—Perfect! says Ariane who is turning her tooth around at the end of the string like a little pearl.

—Will you show me your marbles?

—Oh no, says Ariane confiscating from me the illicit sack. Oh no . . . These ones here are crummy. I will bring you my prettiest ones some other day. And if you like them, you can keep them. But these ones here, they're lame, I swear.

—But . . . I don't want to take your marbles, protests the dentist's wife with that somewhat lost smile that Ariane's speeches invariably provoke in the unsuspecting listener, I was just . . .

—Goodbye, ma'am, Ariane cuts in with as much brutality as ceremony. I thank you very much. Now we gotta go, my mother will be looking for us.

And the dentist's wife, from her doorstep, watches us take off at a gallop, with a very pretty and uncomprehending smile on her lips that didn't have time to fade.

After having turned the corner, I chew Ariane out That's not cool to go telling everybody that your father drinks!

—He's your father too, Ariane shoots back who always latches on to unimportant details each time she's called out for being wrong.

—Even more reason. It makes us look really great.

—It's him who's drinking, says Ariane, not us. Shit. It's not a big deal, is it?

—Exactly. When it's not a big deal, you keep your mouth shut.

Shit, says Ariane. Shit shit shit. Shit.

—And besides we're his family.

—I didn't do it on purpose, says Ariane, leaving it unclear whether she is pleading lack of responsibility for what she said or for being part of that family of ours. So, that flower, you get it, yes or no?

—Sure did! It's fake, totally fake. A mix of nylon fringe, plastic thorns, and little bits of fabric, it's embarrassing. Did you know that?

—And so what Ariane says to me. Who said it had to be real? It just has to be the prettiest flower, and it is.

She takes the flower out of the bag and twirls it in the sun, and it's true that it's the most beautiful flower that you ever saw.

—Do you think she'll notice?

—Who gives a shit, says Ariane. And first of all you don't think she spends her time counting the flowers after each patient leaves, do you? You can be such an idiot!

But this almost certain impunity only made my remorse worse: a woman so beautiful. So sweet. So attentive, even to rascals like us . . .

—It's true, says Ariane her eyes unfocused and the tooth fallen back to the end of the string. It's true, she is nice. You know she told me the true story of the real Ariane? Now I really like that name. And HIM I'm going to tell him to stop his bullshit about cars. You'll see: he'll be blown away, that bum.

The boys had all returned with flowers that were pathetic or wilted or that stank.—Camille wins! trumpeted Ariane. It's Camille's flower that is the prettiest in the woooooooorld! It's Camille who is chosen, so theeeeeere!

—Hey, just a minute, Maurice said, the boy whose flower might have been considered the least ugly. Whoa there! Camille is NOT ABLE to be chosen, for the simple reason that she's a girl . . .

—So what? says Ariane swinging her tooth under the boy's nose as if it were a bicycle chain.

—So nothing. She's a girl.

—Who's denying it? says Ariane, lip curling nose wrinkling in a snarl.

—Uh . . . No one, the boy said confusedly in the middle of the circle of the other brats who were inclined to back him up right or wrong Just, she's a girl. There you go. And she can't be chosen by another girl. Gotta be a boy. Right, Mylene?

—And first of all, says Ariane, is Mylene choosing between boys, girls, or flowers? Which flower do you prefer, Mylene?

—Camille's flower, says Mylene with a certain hesitation, but . . .

—Is it Camille's flower that's the prettiest, yes or no?

—Yes. Yes certainly . . . But . . .

—Grrreat. So it's that flower there that you prefer?

—Yes . . . But.

—Then there is not the least 'but', says Ariane. Catch!

With that, having attached the flower to a pebble with the string from her tooth, Ariane expedites the whole thing, tooth included, right into Mylene's two hands that she held out mechanically.

—That's no fair! clamoured the boys.

Meanwhile, Mylene was contemplating the flower completely befuddled. Just recently, I thought she was really cute, Mylene with her thick, black hair, her pretty little breasts under her dress—she's already almost fifteen—and her laugh that's like her mother's but even prettier. All of a sudden, she seems dull to me, because of some unknown bad light A little stupid, also, I don't know why. I want to take the flower back from her, to give it back to the dentist's wife as if that were possible, or at least to call off this idiotic game, to extract myself from this senseless face-off.

—It's twice as unfair, huffed Maurice, 'cause that flower, it's fake. There's cheatin' going on!

Ariane was going to argue more, or even fight, because she was twiddling her lasso about in a menacing way, when suddenly I've had it.

—Fine, whatever, that's all right. Give me my flower and let's stop talking about it.

And just as my little sister Ariane was turning on me like a fury swinging her lasso like a slingshot I felt myself suddenly soften mentally liquefy and run like a puddle at the feet of a woman beautiful and sweet and laughing like we never see around here and who surely did not deserve to have someone steal a flower from her, even a fake one, to become the object of a quarrel among this bunch of brutes.

—You chicken, my little sister Ariane said who sees everything always but who sometimes misinterprets things. Pathetic! You're a pathetic 'fraidy cat, you disgust me.

And to Mylene, who was still scrutinizing the flower as if some answer would spring from it:

—You too, you disgust me: you're only good for sniffing their muddy flowers, their shitty flowers! C'mon, you give it back to us, it's ours. And go screw yourself. It'll be a long time before we'll bust our ass again for your pretty eyes, you fricking stupid princess bitch!

And since after all my little sister Ariane lost her tooth in the adventure, there is a little corner of blue in the sky and a false bit of sun on the sidewalk, she quickly recovers her good mood and starts belting out her refrain at full volume, balancing on the edge of the sidewalk her arms flung out wide:

'The children oooooof the eaaarth . . .
Have given uuuuuuup on God . . .
They lo-ve each other without a care . . . .
As lovers doooooooo . . .

I loooooove you, you looooove me, we
looooove each other,
Until the end of tiiiiiiime . . .'

The line is free, finally, and I hear Ariane's voice, so strong, as always, that you feel it in your gums. Very far off, there's a clanking of objects knocked over of a child crying who someone consoles by yelling Who is it? WHO? . . . Yes, my baby, but speak CLEARLY, shit, I can't hear a thing. Hold on, hold on, Mama's coming . . . But WHO is speaking, seriously? Oh . . . Oh it's you Camille . . . Hang on a second.

I wanted to hang up, because my little sister Ariane seemed to have evaporated into the ether, only surviving as a memory or a tiny speck, somewhere in space where our old markers no longer show the path. But Ariane's voice returned, unencumbered by parasitical noise, softened or weakened but unmistakably hers, hammering words at full speed as if she feared that someone would cut her off Or as if she had to stuff them in by force in a minimum amount of time and space before God only knows what imminent deadline or catastrophe . . .

—Oh Camille . . . What's happening, is it serious? Listen I'm completely swamped The housekeeper has the flu and she gave it to the baby and on top of everything else Richard . . . No, it's not worth talking about it's too long a story So long story short everything's going to fucking hell in this God-forsaken shack and so . . .

—Ariane. Ariane. Abel is dead.

She said Huh What It was necessary to repeat Dead. Dead, I tell you. She asked if I was sure If I had

SEEN him. If . . . Listen, Camille, don't get mad, but with you . . .

And after she said Shit. Shit then . . . Mama!

'Mama', of course. She didn't say 'Papa'. Not one among us ever said 'Papa' with the ease of words that just flow out, that naturally come out of your mouth. On these two syllables, we trip. They stick Don't pass It's necessary to expel them by force, in case of absolute necessity, when the use of 'him' or of 'he' becomes impossible or rude.

I recognized him in photos, however. At the age of two I apparently would give moving speeches on the subject of this 'little daddy of mine who is in Germany with the Krauts'. Didn't he still resemble the handsome marriage portrait? I forget. I lost interest, the magic word lost en route. Most likely, the word 'papa' for me meant only a piece of glossy paper that I had to kiss to make everyone happy. If he had died, I think I would have ended up loving him a lot. Coming back was his first mistake.

One day he was back. I see my mother on her knees. He was dark everywhere: dark eyes, dark hair, rough dark beard that sprouts on his cheeks from morning to night. He's a man who doesn't know how to smile He is immense and silent He takes up the whole room And when he happens to speak to me, his voice only serves to shatter fragile things in me, and I cry. I push him away I hit him I push him away from my mother, who belongs to me I can't stand when he touches her And in the end I say it to him: Get out! Then he looks at me, with his terrible black eyes, as if he meant to exterminate me on the spot.

I have several memories of my early childhood with my father. Silent for the most part, and always in shadows. As if he darkened the space around him.

Someone knocks on the windowpane in the door. It's my father. I don't look at him. My mother draws my attention She feigns surprise, insists, turns my head in the right direction. As I am forced to look at him, he raises his arms and shows me through the window an immense Puss in Boots that he has just won at the fair. He is not smiling—my father never smiles or laughs—but even still he seems content I remember him by I don't even know what detail, maybe by the way his eyes are looking, or the cheeks, Some minute modification of the physiognomy that escapes me for the moment. I know that the Puss in Boots is for me. It has red boots and a big feather in its hat. But that doesn't interest me. It doesn't interest me, because HE brought it for me.

I don't remember having seen my father come in. Or having touched that prodigious toy, dead on arrival. Or—even more so—having ever played with it. They must have concluded that it scared me, that giant Cat, and discreetly retired it from circulation.

But I can see again very clearly my father immobile behind the glass, proudly holding the Puss in Boots in his arms, looking at me with an air of contentment but without even the slightest smile. A closed image   Frozen   Captured in the mirror. Between him and me, there will always be that glass. For Abel and Ariane, I don't know how it happened.

I killed Papa.

—Again, grumbled my sister Ariane hanging her jacket on the coat hook after having brushed the collar a little with her elbow. What with, and for how long?

For some time now, Ariane has frankly scorned my incompetence at assassination. My attempts, at first superb, shrivelled in her mind to the dimensions of a barely noticeable habit, certainly monotonous and fastidious, that might still achieve a result, but only by the greatest of accidents.

There will always be, from Ariane to me, that ardent surge of enthusiasm, of admiration, of total confidence that lights up the depths of her eyes. Then gradually this light grows dimmer, powering down and finally goes out, the source cut off. Ariane then considers me with a sort of patience worn down by the accumulation of disappointments, until the implacable rising-up of that sideways look that says I knew it It will always be the same thing, and that look which reduces me more and more to the sum of my incompetence.

My little sister Ariane is of an efficient and secure race, who go straight where they need to, who always do what must be done, who despise nothing so much as distraction or failure, and who do not understand how one might in any way hesitate or give up. She has always been precise and balanced like a battle axe.

—I swear to you. I swear to you that this time it's true.

—Every time you swear, gripes Ariane. And every time you mess up.

But this time it's true. I jumped on my bike. There was no one on the banks of the canal, not even a barge on the horizon. Nothing but the reeds, that the wind was shaking, with a very light cracking noise. I pedalled as if I had the Devil on my tail, I came back to the house.

—Papa is dead. I just killed him.

—I don't believe you, said Ariane testing the elasticity of her rubber balls with her thumb. Where is he?

—In the canal.

—You're SURE?

—Yes.

—You're the one who put him in?

—Yes.

For a second, Ariane hesitated:

— . . . Maybe we ought to tell Mom?

I went to tell my mother, who said Where in the canal?

—In the canal. Where we fish.

—He fell in?

—Yes.

—And what did you do? You called for help?

—Uh, nothing . . . Uh no. There wasn't anybody, so.

—Oh crap! said my mother, he's going to catch cold on me, coming back like that all wet . . . I'm calling the firemen.

—But he's IN it.

—Well I hope he's out by now, said my mother. Luckily he knows how to swim. But you never know, with clothes and boots, and as cold as it is . . . If he gets out he's gonna catch pneumonia on me, you don't realize!

—That's really clever, said Ariane as my mother was slamming the door. You already messed up. You didn't know he can swim?

No. I didn't know, no. I saw him coming out of the reeds like a creature from the black lagoon Except a swamp creature doesn't holler doesn't cough doesn't complain Little shits You're all little shits! Vampires! Murderers! I ain't got kids, they're wolves . . .

At first my mother blamed bad luck or my clumsiness, taking my father's certainty for pure and simple obsession. But today I saw that she wasn't so sure any more. And I was seized by a sudden fatigue, like a discouragement in all my limbs. I didn't even know any more why I wanted to kill him so badly. He wasn't really a bad sort, my father. Not even a true tyrant. Only a terrorizing figure in front of whom Abel peed himself out of nervousness—But Abel had nothing to do with the perpetual reckoning of accounts that caused me to try to snuff out my father any chance I got, that at least was sure.—But if I started having second thoughts, I really knew that I was fucked.

On that note, Abel came out of his room, where Ariane had gone, in her own words, to 'let him in on the secret'.

—Where's Mom?

—Dunno. At the firehouse.

—It's true that you killed him, right?

—I don't know any more. Seems he knows how to swim.

—You pushed him in the water?

—Yes, says Ariane. But we're telling you that he's going to come back. He's a man who never dies for good.

Abel shut up. Then he said He's not gonna be happy with what we done . . . Mechanically, I corrected:

—With what we DID. Or rather, with what I did . . .

—WE'RE gonna get balled out, insisted Abel.

—What else is new, said Ariane. You're not going to pull that prank of fainting, are you? Because we're warning you, calmly, in advance.

Abel reflected, then he said that no, as long as we warned him calmly . . . But my father came home in the fire truck (whose sirens had brought the entire neighbourhood to their windows), laid out on a gurney and covered with a big white sheet. And, in shock, Abel became stiff as a pylon whose wires sizzled due to a short circuit. I had just enough time to throw myself between him and the floor, while Ariane, from her window, filled me in:

—He's alive. They didn't pull the sheet up over his face.

My father didn't catch pneumonia. Barely even a real bronchitis, that he recovered from by railing and swearing without however taking time off work.

—He's courageous, said my mother without looking at anyone and as if she were talking to the walls.

No one answered, because she herself didn't expect an answer. But I had had enough of killing my father. All the more so since this time he said absolutely nothing about it, only holding suspiciously still, as though he were burdened by a sort of torment that was far too complicated for him, which he tried to protect himself from by looking away by looking at nothing, the way you keep silent in avalanche zones.

I had the sudden certain knowledge that we were not Avengers but little shits. And I see my father again, who is carrying in his arms a puppy no bigger than his fist. It's a girl puppy, her name is Alaska. My father smiles almost, or at least puts forth what seems to be a little light, seeming to come from nowhere, and which changes his face imperceptibly. The same as that day when he brought home Puss in Boots.

And then immediately after, that other image breaks hacks cuts in pieces and leaves behind an absolute desert. Little Alaska is tied up in the yard, to an enormous kennel. She barks incessantly, at anything, until my mother goes out and unhooks her and cradles her like a baby. Then she shuts up, licking my mother's chin or her earlobe. We pet her. We feel her little tongue on our hands on our eyelids . . . She still smells like a puppy, Alaska. She coos and whines softly We figure out that her kennel is too big, her leash too short and too heavy, and the hard dirt in the yard too cold for the pink and tender pads of her paws. My father doesn't want the dog in the house. It's on principle, says my mother.

—What's that, a principle?

—Oh, says my mother, a thing that doesn't make much sense . . . But what do you do, your father is your father.

At just that moment he comes back in, zigzagging a little as he is wont to do sometimes even then. He is dark, as always, his cheeks black from his beard that is resprouting. Alaska, seeing him, begins to bark as if he was an intruder. My father holds his head, covers his ears with his hands. He has a headache. He always has a headache. The dog barks even louder, and my father explodes: 'Listen, you're going to shut the fuck up!' And since Alaska just barks even louder, even as little as she is, he grabs her by the neck and lifts her up very high, the whole length of her chain. Choking cries from the little dog. The sudden arrival of my mother on the landing from which I was witnessing the scene. She screams 'What are you doing? Robert, you're crazy   Stop! Stop!' and at the same time she makes me go back in the house, her arms around my head. Below, the cries of the puppy have been cut off. Never again would we see little Alaska, whom my father strangled in a fit of anger.

Later, my mother will say about my father   He's a crazy one. But he loved his dog, he's the one who brought her home . . . And then later again, when my mother was chiding my father about the death of Alaska—it was in the context of another dog that he wanted to adopt—my father will get up from his chair with his killer look and his monstrous fists crushing the table as if he were ready to kill again: 'Enough, with that, you hear. You will never bring that up with me again. NEVER!' My mother then shuts up, hugs me in her arms with Abel, turning her back to my father as though to protect us better from his bloody furious look that had fallen on her and us both. And until my father left slamming the door, we stayed pretty much waiting for death all three of us.

Now, my father pets other people's dogs.

To them, he talks a little. Things that are unintelligible to humans. He speaks to them with patience and humility. He touches them with gentleness, as he never touched his children, asserts my mother with a certain bitterness. It's true that us, we avoided him. Dogs didn't.

I tell Ariane that I'm letting it drop. That our father is too hard to kill, that I've had enough. Ariane says only It's just as well You're so inept. And she clomps down the stairs whistling. Abel says nothing. He never says anything. We don't know what he thinks, with his look of being lost among an endless series of walls. When Ariane and I are in two different places, he hesitates no end, not knowing whom to follow. One would say he is perpetually lost in a glass-paned labyrinth, able to see everyone but unable to reach them, like in fairy tales. So he hops back and forth, as if his whole body is split asunder by contrary contortions, and my mother orders whichever of us hasn't cut out yet: 'Take your brother.'

Yes, but this time Ariane isn't there, and me I'm going to the dentist, it's out of the question for me to go escorted by my younger brother, what would I look like? I say this to my mother I'm almost sixteen, jeez! As for him, to be fair, he's not three any more. My mother concedes. Promises Abel to play war with him, while waiting for the return of Ariane who must have still been shooting marbles with her band of hooligans. And she wipes away Abel's sadness, which is total and incomprehensible. She has a big thirteen-year-old baby. The world is shot through with absurdities that my mother refuses to unravel. And me sometimes I would like to sleep—to sleep forever—until I'm at least twenty-five.

Well, hello! said the dentist's wife as I was shutting the door, I think we've met before . . . haven't we?

She was behind the mini-counter, between the plants, filling in for the secretary (a frizzy blond who talks to you without looking at you, for whom I regularly wish a quick death, or marriage, really anything that would get rid of her for us once and for all. The miracle, had it happened?) I was a bit hot in the cheeks because of the flower, but it was such old news—four, five years, already?—and besides there was no other dentist in the neighbourhood.

—Annick is sick?

—Yes, said the dentist's wife without dropping her eyes from mine.

—Uh . . . Is it serious?

—Oh no, I don't think so A flu . . . Is it her that you wanted to see?

I said no not at all on the contrary Well really not exactly the contrary, but . . . Really I mean . . .

She laughed—it was more a laugh than a smile, even though perfectly silent—with her pretty little dimples on each side, unseen for ages and yet never forgotten.

You're going to have to wait a bit, said the dentist's wife still watching me with her big, black eyes as if she knew everything about me and accepted all of it, my husband is busy, he has a difficult case: general anaesthesia. Are you in a hurry?

—No. No, ma'am.

—How is Ariane?

—Oh . . . You remember us?

She laughed again, in silence, the light of the electric bulbs dancing in her large, black eyes:

—Oh! You bet . . . My first extraction. And my husband was absolutely furious, baby tooth or not Said to me Do you realize what you've done! As if I had just revealed to him that there was a dead body under the rug, or something like that . . . You're talking about an epic story, that tooth of your little sister Ariane! How old is she now, Ariane?

—She's twelve.

—Wow! And you?

—Almost sixteen.

—You've grown a lot, changed a lot . . . But you still have that look of not knowing where to stand. I recognized you, but your first name, I've forgotten it . . .

She bit her lip:

—Are you angry with me?

I said no. That my name is Camille. She says I like it, Camille . . . It's . . . very very very wisely androgynous. It suits you well. You know what that means, androgynous?

—Yes, ma'am.

I felt the moment coming when she would have nothing more to say to me, when she would fall silent, go away, leaving me alone with the flowers that were still in the same place on their side table, haunting. Inalterable.

—You know . . . Ariane is still as chatty as ever. Much chattier than I or my brother.

—Oh! You should have brought her, she could have made conversation for us . . . She still plays marbles?

—Yes . . . She also juggles with little balls. She would have overwhelmed us, for sure.

Strange sweetness in the look that is starting to slide to one side however as if mine had pushed against it with too much force. Suddenly I remember the constant injunctions of my mother:

—Stop staring at people. It bothers them. After all, you're not a baby, any more!

I lower my eyes, a little. She has on a blue dress, with a square neckline and sleeves that stop below the elbows. But it's just as bothersome to contemplate a woman's breasts Or her belly-button Or her legs I ask myself WHERE one can safely direct one's gaze So I look at the dentist's wife's hands, which are pretty and solid, and which continue to shuffle the paperwork on the counter.

—That's a little girl with a lot of big ideas, Ariane . . . A lot of personality, no?

—Oh! For sure.

—So you also have a brother?

—Yes.

—Do I know him?

—I don't know ma'am. His name is Abel. He's very handsome, especially his eyes. He's thirteen.

She says that mine are not so bad either As for Ariane's eyes, she can't remember them, she was talking so much. Even with the surgical pliers in her mouth, she was still talking! She looks at her watch She says that she has a bit more time, that I could sit down . . . And I have the feeling that it's completely fucked up, that I was beyond the pale, that she has had enough of such a lame conversation. I lift my eyes up again, and our gazes connect. I must be staring too hard. She had an imperceptible flicker of her lashes, swiftly stilled. Again that silent laugh, those dimples that come and go And then she smells good, not like the Mothers whose cheap eau de cologne stinks from several metres away when they remember to put some on. Me, I refuse to wear any. But maybe I stink, how would I know, in spite of the soap . . .

Very abruptly, I went to sit down on the bench against the wall. The dentist's wife comes out from behind the little counter and I see the whole dress The fragility of her waist and the little swelling of her belly The smooth legs, without the least hair, and tanned . . . I don't feel at all comfortable. As if one of Annick's microbes, left behind on the countertop, had jumped on me.

Meanwhile, she says to me, with that troubling sweetness which seems so natural to her, that it will be at least another half hour That I'm the last one, there are no more appointments for this evening, and would I like some tea?

That smile—big, silent laugh that comes at you, as though projected, as one would blow a kiss—it's over, I will never be able to get rid of it It entered into my body and I know that day and night I will carry it, like a really little knife, like a minuscule burn . . .

—I . . . I don't know, ma'am. I never drank any.

—My name is Clara, said Clara. Come, we'll go see if you don't like my tea. It's Russian tea, it's very good.

We leave the waiting room, me scraping my feet on the carpet as much as possible to wipe my soles in case they weren't too clean . . . There was such a commotion inside my skull that I am struck deaf and dumb I bang my shoulder into the door frame, and it's Clara again who rubs it, as though she were at fault, as if she were responsible for the narrowness of the door, while I find nothing to say absolutely nothing at all that might give the slightest hint of intelligence underneath the stupidity that I am mired in, and from which I hope with all my heart to have the strength to break out of by running . . .

Finally, I don't know how, I am seated. At a pretty table with a tablecloth and a bouquet of anemones. Making sure that I can't knock anything onto the floor with my elbow, then I stop thinking. I look at the decor: lots of books, on shelves. That calms me down a little. Clara during this time busies herself in the kitchenette with the noise of the gas and the cups.

—You want some music? You like music?

God in Heaven! What should I respond? It's surely classical music that she's proposing. In school, they made us listen to one or two pieces that weren't bad, but I forgot all the titles. If I say 'no', I'll sound like a barbarian. If I say 'yes' she's going to ask me what. And if I clam up, it's impolite.

—Oh, you're looking at my books . . . You can go look at them closer, you know. You read a little?

Her, she's a woman of superior intelligence. I say that I read, yes, quite a bit. She can even ask me what, I am infinitely less afraid in that domain. But one question tortures me: what is that odour that I smell on myself? Burnt coffee? Soap? Sweat? While Clara goes back to find the teapot, I sniff under my arms surreptitiously. Nothing. Just the wool of my sweater. But you can't smell yourself, everyone knows that. Be sure to keep your distance, in any case. I'm standing in front of the books, but all the titles run into one another, because not only is my head scrambled but my vision as well.

—Come, says Clara, tea's ready. I can lend you some books, if you want. You just have to choose something a little later.

Smile received smack in the face. Dimples. My brain turns to mush. And before me Clara's arms, sheathed in blue to just below the elbow, that are serving me tea.

—Lemon?

I nod yes. She serves herself as well. Lemon for both of us. I hate lemon, but this is surely how things are done.

—If you don't like it, says Clara, don't drink it. I'll make you a hot chocolate. So, you read a lot?

I drink. I burn myself stoically. Except that it's boiling hot, the taste is bearable, lightly vomitous. In the end, I like the smell, that's something.

—Are you okay, Camille? You like it, after all?

—Yes, ma'am.

She says again, with the same smiling patience as if it were the first time: My name is Clara.

And suddenly he comes in like a gust of wind:

—Oh! Here you are. I just called an ambulance, this fellow's not waking up normally. I'm going with him, I'll feel better if I do. You'll cancel the appointments?

She gets up quickly, asks if it's serious.

—No . . . Well, I don't think so. But I prefer . . . So you . . .

—There are no more appointments, says Clara. Just Camille, whom I was making wait, as you see. But surely she can come back. You can come back?

I say yes, of course. The dentist disappears with a banging of the door, after having glanced my way in passing and showing me his upturned palms to signal his apologies.

The tea is finished. Clara is preoccupied. I slide out quickly, without having chosen any books since I am coming back tomorrow. I'm putting you down for the last appointment, says Clara, so that we can have time for the books. Okay? I'm feeling a little too nervous, now. You're not angry with me?

As I leave I pay attention to the door frame, but I get caught up on the floor mat of the waiting room. Clara catches me vigorously by the collar. She laughs, and I want to die, right then and there, until she caresses my cheek with the back of her hand still laughing:

—I think I've never met someone so distracted! Goodbye, Camille . . . See you tomorrow.

She took my hand in hers, with a slightly imprecise movement of her whole body She cast her smile into my face And her gaze imperceptibly shivered in mine, I didn't turn away quickly enough.

When she had shut the door, I sort of hugged the walls while walking because frankly I felt unwell—the tea? the lemon? or that smile that was still almost gentle even as it turned in my flesh like a very little knife?—

—Oh, my God! says my mother, you look so strange. He hurt you?

—No. He couldn't see me. There was a sick patient, he took him to the hospital. I have to go back there tomorrow.

—What was wrong with the other patient?

—I don't know. They took him away in an ambulance, the doctor with him.

—How ridiculous, says my mother, you're so impressionable . . . You want some lemon water with a sugar cube?

I said that I didn't want anything. That I had a toothache, a helluva pain. That I didn't want to eat either. That I was going straight to bed.

My mother felt my forehead, decided that in fact it would be wise and that she would make me some bouillon. I laid down. I sprang up like a shot to go throw up the tea with lemon. Then I fell asleep so soundly that my mother, after a few tries, gave up on waking me.

That night, and also the next day, my mother worried as patiently and painstakingly as if I had disappeared in a faraway land. Mothers detect things, even if they misunderstand them. And mine, who knows nothing, always truly knew at what exact moment her children one after another abandoned her.

II

'It's like the other madness, the mad wish to know, to remember, one's transgressions.'

S. Beckett (*The Unnamable* 68)

Abandoned. Always the grand words. Did Ariane herself 'abandon' her? In spite of the undeniable way things appear, I can't quite manage to believe it. As for Abel, who was never with anyone, he seemed well rooted, if not to my mother, at least to the geometric space defined by her and dislocation from it profoundly rattled him. And even me, what am I doing here except waiting for her to come back, she who among all the Mothers who don't kill themselves would today have reason to kill herself, or to kill me, or both of us together because we live in any case in a world of cries of furore and foolishness.

Foolishness so obvious, sometimes, that I ask myself if the Mothers' conversation doesn't have an underlying function that they themselves aren't aware of. If they don't secrete that particular form of fog to drown to erase to retract all sharpness or particular brilliance apt to serve as a lightning rod. If they don't do it, even unconsciously, as an exercise in camouflage . . . They have their folklore, made of memories held in common, their timid uncertainties, their shared ignorance of how the world works, and a fanatic anxiety about blending into the background, to not 'stand out'. As if the misery that lies in wait was alert to the least bit of originality.

So they rehashed their memories, as if life was woven of nothing but current drudgery and past good times, and no one can follow their stories about the war or about what came before it any more, the additions and subtractions from one version to the next contradict themselves so much. It's as if they don't know very well themselves, distanced as they are in the tortuous turns of events, what happened, there, right under their noses, while they were young, as they say. Except for the bombings, the exodus and the underground dances that took place even during the bombardments, their History, for them it's Chinese almost as much as for us, except for Gertrude who used to be German . . . So much so that on Liberation Day a few hotheads claimed she was a spy and that she ought to have her head shaved.

—They shaved her? panicked Ariane.

No, no, says Margot, that would've been the last straw! She had surely slept with at least one Kraut, Gertrude, but since it was before the war and when she was still German it didn't count. General agreement from the Mothers. And besides that, my mother adds on, there were those who had a reason to whitewash themselves because of the black market.—That must have been awful, says Abel who is terrified of black.—So the men from the neighbourhood, my father at the head of the pack made it clear to them that they had to go shave somebody else, because not everyone was dead no joke, and if we were really going to keep score, who knew who would end up shaved . . . This is how Gertrude kept her beautiful hair, which had quite a few men running after her, notes Micheline with a certain tightening of her mouth, and kept her job at the factory.

Then they hear Gertrude coming in, and they change the conversation. They had enough time, in any case, since she stopped to play cootchie-coo with somebody's baby, just outside Margot's window.

Despite the half-jokes that she bombarded pregnant women with, Gertrude views other women's babies with a sort of gluttony. She takes them in her arms kisses them nibbles on them One might say that she stops just short of chomping down through the skin and sucking the bones and the marrow. Then her eyes are very sombre and heavy and focus on something no one else can see. And when Mylene happens to be present at these scenes of cannibalism, having for once escaped the chores and atonements that make up her days, she is stiff like a dead little body that someone had forgotten standing against the wall.

Gertrude also has flights of nostalgia when she speaks about the Black Forest. Then her sombre gaze falls upon the first kid who wanders into her field of vision, and she promises, in her soft gluttonous voice One day . . . One day I will take you into the Black Forest with me. If I win the sweepstakes I swear to you I'll take you there. You'll see how beautiful it is . . .

—No! yells Abel with the flicker of a short circuit already in the depths of his eyes   No I won't go with you to your Black Forest   No I won't go, no!

—Gee he's really stupid this little one, Gertrude complains with the air of someone who had just been jolted awake   My God, he's really dumb. The Black Forest, it's not black at all, if that's what's got your panties in a twist. It's green. With immense trees, and a silence . . . A silence you can't even imagine, especially when there's snow. That's when you practically smell it, like a fragrance . . .

—I won't go! Abel insists glued like paper to the wall. I won't go. I won't go.

—Course not, you won't go, assures my mother. Don't be afraid . . .

Then Gertrude's gaze comes to rest on mine with a sort of gentleness as though looking for somewhere to land A sort of light trepidation or a supplication:

—And you, Camille? You won't come either?

I feel something like pity for that gaze in search of who knows what ambiguous consent, what murky understanding. I say yes, I would come. Sure I would go, yes, with Gertrude, to breathe the silence of her Black Forest and to walk in the snow. And I get the impression very brief—and very obscure—of having been cornered into promising something that seems like sharing a death . . . Luckily, they never win, with their damn sweepstakes tickets which they barely won back the face value of on their luckiest days.

—Why don't you take your daughter instead? suggests my mother as if from outside and nevertheless without breaking open this sort of hermetic silence—like a spell, a strange and smooth peace beyond time—that has closed around Gertrude and me since my promise, enclosing us in the same invisible bubble in the midst of the small talk of the others of the sounds of the cups of the smell of boiled coffee and the smoke of the caramel-scented cigarettes.

When Gertrude's gaze finally lets me go—tears itself from the invisible bog into which it had sucked me and itself—I have something like a layer of cold around my bones, but I feel an intense comfort from it.

Then I hear my mother who's talking about school and about my report card 'Overactive imagination', the French teacher wrote in the margin. My mother wonders if that is a compliment or a reproach, and looks at me with suspicion. Eh? Whatta you think?

I say cagily that I don't know. The other mothers, consulted, don't know either but it doesn't seem like a big deal to them, even if it is a reproach. All the same, mine is still on guard:

—It wouldn't be, by any chance, that you're STILL telling tales?

The trouble is, my mother has the memory of an elephant. She will never forget.

'Very good student', the school mistress had written when I was eight, 'even though a little timid at speaking. Ought to wear glasses. Fabricates maybe a little?'

—She fabricates, my mother had said to the eye doctor handing him my report card to back up what she was saying. Need to fix that.

Well-mannered people don't burst out laughing They have a tight little smile A look that skips around you as if you were questionable And they explain that that has nothing to do with glasses in the same flat voice that they use to explain the breakdown of the bill.

—Oh good, said my mother caught off guard but not completely deflated, me, you know, I'm not real knowledgeable.

And to me, in the street, after having ruminated over the episode a bit:

—All the same . . . I hold her accountable, your school mistress. They shouldn't mix everything up like that. And you, do you realize you made me look like an idiot? Why do you tell tales?

From then on, I wear glasses. It's as though the scenery has been scrubbed. Every detail, with frightening precision, forces its way into my brain and remains planted there. And at the same time the world is cold Suddenly distant polished sanitized I see it through this glass I see it far away, out of reach It's as though I'm withdrawn from it, excluded, or at least SEPARATED.

Much later, I will read *Les Animaux dénaturés*—those who left nature and who observed it from outside—and I'll know that me too I'm something that's been DENATURED A unit that doesn't have a place, no stable morphology, nor status nor security.

But it's between eight and nine years old that I came unstuck from the world—or rather, that it was detached from me in order to be presented to me as a spectacle—and ever since I have been vainly seeking how to re-enter it and blend in, how to get back through the glass.

The Mothers are worried about the Black Jackets, of which it seems there is a gang in the neighbourhood.—It's more likely the Tiny Jackets, judges Ariane who has already had some words with them about marbles—In point of fact no one really knows much about them, except unsubstantiated rumours that claim they escaped from a new, neighbouring housing project where they were beginning to get bored after having broken up entrance doors stair rails fences and other stuff street lamps barely installed, where they tore out twisted off ripped apart chopped down and finally burnt all the trees bushes and shrubs that had the bum luck to be planted there, and even went so far as to stomp back into the dust even the tiniest blade of grass that dared to sprout around the sandboxes converted into fighting rings before ending up as spittoons and shit holes.

—My oh my, lament the Mothers, it's hardly worth having gotten rid of the Krauts to . . .

Gertrude shuts up so awkwardly that they finally remember that she used to be German, and that it isn't done any more to talk of 'Jerrys' and of 'Krauts' since the Americans came over and flattened them, helped at the other end of the earth by the Russians, and they destroyed them all to the relief of the nations. Bastards, for sure, but polite. You never woulda guessed, just looking at them But as for these, Jesus Mary! Rotten trash. Local boys—And so, drawls Gertrude, trash, there's ones like that everywhere—They talk just like us but they act like they're in Chicago . . .

The Mothers know Chicago like the back of their hand, from the movies. The gang does too probably. The eldest among them even start to scar their faces with bicycle chains because that's the trend now.—Which strikes mortal fear of the Black Jackets in Abel, what with him already disliking black.—Soon, it'll be like America here . . .

But that America, we don't give a crap about it, objects Ariane who doesn't let herself be impressed by others' assertions, it's not our America. And she clamps on her lasso. Which is starting to annoy my mother, because Ariane has grown up a lot.

Ah! But you don't know what they've come up with, Margot says to Gertrude, it's unbelievable! For three days under my windows I've had a row of guys pissing. They've been having a contest on height, imagine that. And the more I threw water on them, the more they came to piss. And with insults that I wouldn't even dare to repeat!

My mother turns away, but Gertrude openly convulses with laughter. Micheline is, as always, lifeless and blue. Margot's cheeks, crumpled like old tissue paper, are still trembling. Luckily Micheline's Larbi, injured by a miracle as sometimes happens, found himself with his arm in a cast and free time for napping. Woken up with a start by the braying of the guys pissing and Margot's shouts, in a bad mood because of his arm four times heavier than usual, he went down the stairs in two bounds, cradling his arm which was all swaddled up like a baby, and without warning distributed a flurry of kicks with his boots on the pairs of buns that were lined up as if saluting the flag. The thugs, knocked down and befuddled by this reversal, gathered up all their members including the leader and disappeared like grasshoppers in a big cloud of dust. No one had seen them since.

—Let's hope they're gone for good, says Gertrude wiping her eyes.

—Ah! says Micheline wiping her never-ending tears in her rolled-up handkerchief, better to have girls than boys, these days. What worries!

Yeah, Ariane says to me dragging on her Carambar like Margot on her cigarette, but girls, they run risks too . . .

—Just have to keep 'em at home, reckons Abel who likes what Ariane and I call our 'parrot shows'.

— . . . Sometimes, Ariane says with a sombre air, they end up having to work the streets . . . Come to think of it, what's that mean, 'working the streets'?

—No idea.

—You don't want to tell me, right. How do they work the streets?

—I'm telling you I don't know anything about it.

—Fine, says Ariane in a conciliatory tone, I'll find out, and I'll tell you.

Sometime later, one night Ariane woke me up to tell me what she found out about working the streets. It happens on the sidewalk—hence the danger of sidewalks, which the Mothers lived in fear of seeing their daughters end up on—at night. That's all that Ariane was able to learn, except that it 'made money' and that it could get you out of working. I grumbled that first of all I was tired, and secondly anything that could get you out of working is dangerous or dishonest or both at the same time, ask Mom, you'll see. And I resumed my dream in mid-stream, because the warning was clear. The little man in black was always the same or strangely familiar: most often mute and immobile, always neutral, uninvolved, and I would swear all things considered that he had no opinion. An impassive spectator, maybe distracted before whom I unwind tangles of explanations each more absurd and nebulous than the last which seem like justifications or excuses in which I muddle myself because I sense that I'd do better to shut up it'd be smarter and more dignified What do I need his approval for. Besides he never gives it to me nor his disapproval either . . .

—You sleeping? asks Ariane shaking me.

—Yes, shit.

. . . But it doesn't matter I'm laying it on thick even at the risk of sinking slowly into ridiculousness as if I were becoming bogged down mired Without actually stopping in my sluggish progression: the disastrous and vain attempt to convince him of my good faith in which he didn't bother pretending to believe nor to disbelieve He has his own idea I don't know which that nothing will shake . . .

— . . . big dummy! Ariane grouses from the depths of a very dark funnel where I vaguely hear her turning over.

. . . So well that in the end by dint of defending myself against a mistake or bad intention or supposed blunder not to say imaginary By putting on airs, by playing the flirt, by playing the innocent and I don't know what else I end up disgusting myself suspecting myself embarrassing myself and giving myself a guilty conscience, the way you can make yourself itchy by scratching for no reason just for something to do . . .

I tell my dreams to Ariane, who never listens to anything in the morning because she's still groggy, which is perfectly suited to the nature of my outpourings   Which would seem more like verbal fixations than actual confidences.

Before, I remember, there was no little black man with his air of knowing me by heart no matter what I do and not caring a whit   Before there was one or a few cops who followed me everywhere and well they could always run I wouldn't speak and besides I was innocent I didn't even know what they wanted of me really   But in any case I erased the traces I stole the clues and they could always follow me if they wanted it'd be a waste of their time. Obviously, this was no way to live and I would much rather have been calm and been left alone for once, but I was little and you can get used to anything . . .

—You're talkin' my ear off, says Ariane scratching her head and rubbing her eyes, stop . . .

. . . I don't remember any more at what point in my life the cops disappeared   I didn't pay attention it didn't hit me it appears that they slipped away quietly . . .

—Shit, says Ariane in a doleful tone, stop.

. . . And then came the little black man Not all the time but from time to time and the funniest thing is that it's me who always goes first, who speaks and who explains and who enters into hair-splitting details to shed some light God knows what in order to prove my innocence of which the least one could say is that it no longer shines like new . . . By means of convoluted polite phrases despicably 'reasonable' grimaces and other kowtowing performances I try to entice him so he'll respond to me or at least look at me or at least pretend to but no dice. He's silent Looks elsewhere with a humiliating persistence isn't fooled won't take never took will never take sides. Neither for nor against.

The warning was clear. I always wake up with this certainty. But clear for whom?

Oh! You bore me stiff, Ariane explodes, with your dreams. Lemme drink my coffee, shit, I'm not awake . . .

And she flings the window open, while below the big horse known as Marie-who-has-two-sexes scrapes her broom coarsely in the gutter.

The scraped-out gutters give off a scent of sludge, of nasty muck spread out, smeared, encrusted on the cement and drying there. It's summer.

Now we're in October. The leaves in the gutters make just a minuscule crunching sound very slow, very patient, or maybe it's me who comes up with it. But that other day, it was summer.

—No way, you're in love, my little sister Ariane had determined. Ooh la la! It's as simple as ABC, this story, I can tell. But are you doing it on purpose or what? Why her, and not a boy like everyone else? Or shit then, why not an unmarried girl, at least . . .

—Does she? my little sister Ariane finally asked me after a lengthy head-scratching.

I shrugged.

—Gotta know what you want, said Ariane with that implacable and precipitous delivery that always left you with a migraine   Because you're in love or you're not in love and if you're in love there's no discouraging you or otherwise what's love good for   And what is it, huh, if it breaks down at the first bump in the road? Besides Ariane said it remains to be seen, she's the one you stole that flower from, remember? Stuff like that, it always means something   And all that for a cunt who didn't even want it   You should have given it back to her, it was a sign, now it's completely fucked   Oh, come on, pull yourself together, good God! What are we gonna do?

—Are you sure, at least? Ariane insisted with a suspicious look. Seriously, the woman is old, at least twenty-five twenty-six . . . Maybe even thirty, since it's been a while. You realize that?

I didn't have the least desire to discuss it with Ariane. I shrugged my shoulders again. But underneath I was vaguely happy all the same that someone knew, felt my pain, and might possibly fight it.

Ariane rummaged in her pocket, foisted a caramel on me, stuck another one in her cheek, and took me by the hand as if to lead me somewhere—Let's go I won't let you screw up. But boy can you be complicated, my poor Camille, to say the least . . .

—For me, Ariane was saying, it's simple: I'm gonna marry a rich guy and live in a house like you see in the movies, with a manicured lawn a pool and goldfish and curved staircases And I won't lift a finger all day long except to try on new clothes tell the kids stories and maybe go dancing . . . Why don't you do like me? Women, they never have a good job. Even for men it's rare . . .

—And will you love him, your rich guy?

—Maybe, says Ariane after a moment of reflection. You think that richness gets in the way? Anyway, said Ariane with a grand sweeping gesture of her free hand, women who don't love their husbands any more have lovers, that's not a problem.

And since I remained silent:

—You ought to give her a present, concluded Ariane, that'll help. But I wonder what, we're flat broke.

Then my little sister Ariane went off to do the dishes, bellowing, with a force equal to that which she brought to scrubbing the pots:

'The lo-vers from Haaa-vre
Don't neeed the seeea . . . '

While I plunge into a new book, without worrying about the foreseeable bad mood of my mother who on coming back from her errands will send me to wash my hair, and step on it, because if you keep that up we're gonna be late, the one night your father decides to go out And Abel, at least, did he wash? Dear God, what did I do to deserve such mollycoddled kids!

I don't know if I'm 'weak' or just half open, knocking vaguely on I don't know which double, indefinite universe, like a door left ajar that would hesitate endlessly between opening up or shutting tight.

Clara's books, almost surreptitiously, revealed spaces that I could not see in their entirety As if I were lacking a certain sort of light, without even knowing for sure what was missing: the wrong kind of light? Or not enough?—As if I were looking, through a narrow peephole, at the interior of rooms invaded by shadows. And what moves in there, gets up, passes into patches of more or less clarity before disappearing like an illusion, THAT attracts and fascinates me, coming back even in my dreams, rising up, falling back, while I pursue it with a strange gaze as if deprived of eyelids that comes to me while sleeping.

About these books—which very probably were not 'age appropriate'—I speak to no one. Besides, who would care: for my mother, Gertrude, Margot and their group, a book is a book Respectable and superfluous object on which it's not too acceptable to waste one's time when one has adult concerns, but which has the advantage of immobilizing children who are too fidgety and of keeping girls at home when they are at the age of 'running around'. They ask me distractedly if 'it's good?', immediately put off by the number of pages without any pictures. My mother gets impatient only occasionally, when her orders or questions get through to me after too long a time lapse—Hey! I'm talking to you. Sometimes I wonder if you're still alive on the planet, with your Goddamn books. Camille, are you listening to me, yes or no? —

I bring Clara's books back to her. I borrow other ones from her, not paying too much attention to her suggestions, which were timidly offered, anyway. When one of them seems particularly tough or maybe racy to her, she hesitates, her gaze dark, profound, descending in me like a sounding so intimate that I felt absolutely naked, surrendered, dissolved . . .

Sometimes she gives in, as if pushed back by the strength of my arguments. Sometimes she tries to explain it to me first.

—Please . . . I don't like when someone explains it to me.

She doesn't insist, her large, sombre eyes grow bigger by a sort of stumbling consideration As if her gaze encounters an unexpected harshness or upright barrier in me Wall Stone Cliff We don't know As if she were examining a fact that was new and disconcerting because of its indefinite nature but that would hold her strangely at a distance, even as her smile grew larger, perpetually guaranteeing that none of all of this is irreconcilable That we will end up understanding each other after these sudden wind-shifts That we will come together again in some peaceful land, when I'll have become less brutal, sanded, polished by the things of the mind, softened by her steadfast patience.

Sometimes she tries again when I bring her back the books, proposing to 'discuss' them. But we don't know how to talk to each other yet You would think we hadn't read the same book And the light that she shines there, when I happen to let her, strips things down until they're completely eliminated, to the unbearable transparency of glass against glass against a multitude of other glasses behind which there would be nothing . . . Clara reads like Ariane used to squint her eyelids: to make the world disappear.

Because Ariane claims that she's able to make walls disappear or really any object, just by looking at them from a certain angle. She says that then things become transparent and evaporate.

—If it's transparent, tell me what's behind it.

—There's nothing! Ariane becomes impatient considering me with the same irritation as if I were incurably absent-minded or dim-witted. Nothing at all It's transparent-transparent.

—But behind the transparency . . .

—You can't see anything at all! Ariane insists tapping her foot, everything is transparent, everything. It's empty space. Are you stupid, or what?

Ariane wasn't lying. When she lies I know it. I looked at the white and grey and ochre stones of the wall That terrifying solidity of things that Ariane could dissolve with a simple squinting of her eyelids I broke into a light sweat, I felt a pang of nausea unable to be pinpointed that rolled and heaved between my shoulders and my knees . . .

—Stop! Stop it right now. If you pull that with me I'll smack you upside your head.

Ariane stopped. Her gaze on my skin would go back to being normal light inoffensive. I didn't feel foolishly menaced any more with transparency with dissolution with . . . Ariane would only say Poor Camille, what a scaredy-cat, you're afraid of everything, it's unbelievable.

Clara reads like Ariane squints her eyelids: to conquer the haunting presence of things, to deny their absurd consistency, if need be to dissolve it by an excess of brightness. She reads, armed with explanations that come from having read. She conquers the book by sweeping it under the spotlight, like one conquers tenacious dust by attacking it with the appropriate tools You see, here it's very clear . . . I close myself hermetically to Clara's reasoning the way I do to my mother's periodic cleaning fits which transform our room into an uninhabitable wasteland You see, at least it's a little cleaner . . . Is it really necessary that all be 'clear' and 'clean', all shadow dust scraps of paper trace of existence definitively exterminated?

So many people can't put up with the least fogginess the least ambiguity: a scouring is indispensable to them, an immediate explanation is owed them—even if they have to fabricate it themselves in haste and incoherence, or worse yet: to throw themselves without a second thought onto the first one that is presented to them.—

Very quickly I return to that peephole through which, between one book and the next, the single seemingly lidless eye watches as in me rise move sink or float forms both imprecise and charged with mysterious meaning—still unreadable but, I feel it, incessantly on the verge of being not revealed but very slowly approached.—

And because I watch the things moving and imperceptibly changing form, I'm called 'slowpoke' and absent-minded. When my mother is in a good mood, she just says 'how calm!' I'm not calm at all, clouds of particles are traversing me at every moment at lightning-fast speeds. It's precisely because of the speed at which things traverse me, each distinct though torrential, that I'm slowed down: I must constantly survey them and list them, tirelessly 'be up to date' on some personal list for clearing out the chaos. And this type of machine in me, that incessantly registers analyses and verifies and classifies, doesn't allow itself to be slowed down by trivial events.

In this sense, it's doubtless true that I have more time to 'waste' than the average person around me.— Even Ariane has always lived in fear of having 'to catch up' with something: the listener she suspected of wanting to run off before she had finished her sentence, the balls she throws anywhere, the bus that takes off (there'll be another one along in five or ten minutes!), a stitch that pulls out, or even strangers walking ahead, really anything that one could 'catch' or that's 'lacking' as if one's whole life was nothing more than a perpetual high-speed chase . . . —

Me, inexplicably, I have time. I feel it swelling in me and overflowing, endlessly. I give some I lose some I take some And if I lack some, for some ridiculous task, I'll find the time a little later on, it's a question of rhythm.

—You'll slow down on your deathbed! says Gertrude to my mother with a philosophy that she herself would do well to practise.

Because they chat as if their skirts were on fire, half sitting and burning their tongues on the boiling hot coffee, until some greater emergency stuns them and scatters them in pursuit of a plan to deal with the imminent catastrophe: such as the men's return home, as regular as an electric clock, and yet seemingly perpetually unpredictable.

In any case that day it wasn't worth killing ourselves to get out the door faster: my father woke up with a headache, and we didn't go out. Don't make noise, said my mother dropping aspirins into a glass of water, your father has a headache.

He always had a headache He works all day (and sometimes all night too) in the din of sheet metal that they shake that they weld that they hammer and that they stamp. He crawls inside the boilers of ships, climbs to the top of cranes He has on his skin the hot the cold the sea water.

In the bars, afterward, he drinks an illusion of warmth in the company of other bearded spectres And he always has a headache, always.

So when the little dog began to bark and no one could shut her up, something enormous exploded in him He went crazy He would've killed a child—one of us—in the same way, anything just to stop the howling inside his skull, the sounds stabbing like needles into his brain.

Honest folk would have gazed in horror upon his shackled hands on the front page of the newspaper—enormous hands, hard like claws, encrusted with grime that resists even pure bleach—All men like my father have the hands of an assassin. It's why they hide them in their pockets on their days off, not knowing what to do with them otherwise, how else could they protect the fragile clean furnishings of a space in which they don't really belong.

Abel had taken his own hands just like those, exactly the same, to the construction sites where he would cry at age fourteen because it was so cold. The others made fun of him, offered him wine to drink. Abel didn't like wine. Nor those brutal men who would hit him in the ribs as a sign of camaraderie. Nor the stone and the cement that would make his fingers bleed. Nor anything. And now Abel is dead.

—And what's it like, when you're dead? my little sister Ariane had asked.

—It's like when you sleep, says my mother. Except that you don't wake up any more.

—That's not so bad, Ariane had said in a voice that was uncertain all the same. Never ever?

—No. Never ever.

Afterwards Ariane didn't want to sleep any more. Didn't want me to turn out the light any more Or else I had to hold her hand.

—Hold me tighter, you're letting go. I KNOW you're going to let go.

—Hey listen! My hand is cramping. And besides I'm tired. Sleep.

—Then look at me, Ariane would say in the dark. You looking at me?

—Yes. Yes, I'm looking at you. Sleep.

My head turned towards Ariane's bed, I was getting a crick in my neck.

—You're not looking at me any more!

—I am so looking at you.

—Liar!

Ariane was sobbing. I had to turn on the light again. To hold her hand again. To swear that we would wake up, that it was true true, shit! Going to bed became an exercise in synchronization that the least batting of an eyelash could compromise, that the slightest cough would ruin.

After several weeks, Ariane having verified that she kept on waking up normally, the tragedy came to an end, calmly. Reasonably.

At heart, Ariane has always belonged to the race of the Mothers, if one could consider that a consolation. At least she gave warning signs. The Mothers tremble at a future misfortune on the distant horizon. Ariane contemplated her own death, far away, with horror. And then death that doesn't come any closer remains an uncertain shadow after all. The misfortune that waits quietly can maybe be put off until tomorrow. It's on the horizon, sure, but faraway. Here, in the little corner we live in, nothing moves. Just have to be careful. Like a stone. Just don't move a muscle, or as little as possible. Just be deaf and dumb, buried already, barely alive. Reasonable.

I should have been reasonable too Stayed on the beaten path Never opened a book or a door Never looked to one side or through the cracks. Or else I should have killed myself, like Ariane, like the Mothers, little by little, so that it would be already done.

Where we come from only dangerous nuts stick out, standing upright in open country. Abel was a dangerous nut. He died. And me I'll die again and again and again, without ever being able to close my eyes, until the end of time.

—How'd it happen? Ariane finally asks at the end of an interminable silence.

And then Ariane's shouts, shooting through my brain, exploding there like rockets like bullets:

—Oh no! Ariane was saying, not this again.

— . . . Listeeeen! Ariane was yelling into the telephone.

She was talking to me in bursts, like a submachine gun   Listeeeen! Get it into your head that we're not kids any more   How many times did you kill Pop, huh? How many times, before you decided that he would die just fine on his own   How many times have you . . . No but, this is incredible, you . . .

—I'm telling you that I killed Abel.

—Stop, Ariane was yelling, you're going to make me crazy. Not a word, do you hear, I don't believe a word of it! . . . Besides you will never kill anyone, my poor Camille It's a hallucination A thing that gets inside your head . . . Listen, I don't have time for this I'm in a hurry I . . . Listen, Camille . . .

Listen, Camille, you're all out of time, now's the time, make up your mind, shit!

Ariane pushes me pulls me steers me, those times when I change my mind after all the trouble we've gone to The right street, the right sidewalk . . . Just as we're approaching the goal, I balk:

—Okay, lemme go now. There's no danger I'll get lost! What if she sees us, what would I look like?

—Like what you are, sighs Ariane tugging maternally on the hemline of my duffel coat to stop it from riding up in the back. Stand up straight. Like a big oaf Don't back down, eh, Ariane threatens again sticking her index finger up under my ribs like a revolver, otherwise I'll go speak to her, me, to YOUR Clara Because this is really getting . . .

Ariane probably continues her soliloquy to herself, it's one that would hammer the inside of your brain, but since she was getting further away without turning around happily I don't hear it any more. I'm seventeen and everybody finds me 'retarded', from the Mothers who congratulate me on my 'seriousness' with that air that people put on to downplay the significance of a handicap, to my little sister for whom my status quo with Clara is suffocating and who always tries to blast her way out of deadlocks.

Clara's big black eyes and smile got bigger, she embraced me with such lightness that I felt absolutely nothing Said Oh . . . For me? But why . . .

—Because I looove you! bellows Ariane while theatrically pantomiming pulling out her hair and stamping the ground with her foot. It was now or never Seriously don't you pay attention when we go to the movies? I-love-you. It's no big speech, that, you could spit it out without a stammer and putting the right tone to it. I love you, Ariane says in a tragic tone to show me. Like that. There. And then afterwards if she were to take it badly, you could always cry leave dignifiedly fall to your knees or faint, I dunno. But at least SAY IT. Let's GET ON with it. Chicken! Pitiful! And so, what did you do?

Nothing. Strictly speaking nothing. I feel ridiculous. And then shit.

—Ri-di-cu-lous, said Ariane with contempt (mimicking my mother), that never killed anyone. And her, wha'd she do?

Nothing special. She unwrapped it She said it was pretty She put it on the edge of a piece of furniture

She was sweet and attentive, like always. If Ariane thinks it's so easy, with a woman so maddeningly POLITE . . .

—I told you so, pointed out Ariane. Just gotta love a boy if you don't want to put yourself out there At least with them you just gotta wait, because they're the ones who have to talk, it's not a problem.

—Whereas here, Ariane rages after having kicked around a fair number of stones, we're in unfamiliar territory Never before seen Anyway one of you has gotta make up her mind, good God!

—It was all for nothing! Ariane finally sighed after silently chewing on her cheek in a moment of reflection. And now we're broke again. What are we gonna do?

I said to Ariane that WE would not do anything at all That Clara wasn't an idiot, and that she didn't love me, it was rather obvious. And that, even if I still had some doubts, oh well I would figure out on my own some way to clear them up.

—Oh, surely, Ariane said shrugging her shoulders. We can count on you . . .

—Besides, whether she loves me or not, she'll finally SEE.

—My opinion, says Ariane, is that she'll see nothing at all: she's a pro at being blind.

In the end, worn out, confused, I made it clear to Ariane that from now on she was to mind her own business.

—As you wish, said Ariane playing around with her marbles that she was never without since she had given up the lasso. As you wish. But if I were you I'd think twice Because you'll always be alone, my friend And that's no fun when you're sad . . .

After Ariane's departure, I went up to our room to put away the new books I lay down without having opened them, my face under my pillow. My eyes were burning My whole body was burning, as if turning to ash from the inside I didn't even have enough strength for the painful contemplation of these strange forms that were haunting the half-light.

If I still don't know the nature of what I glimpsed through the crack, at least I know that I can expect neither security nor rest of any kind from it: it's not a series of rooms like I had thought at the beginning, but chasms.

Abel is in another sort of abyss, he who just turned fourteen. He's as big as one of those shrubs that they used to plant in the neighbourhood in the middle of iron wire cages, and as skinny. At school, never did one damn thing except mind his manners and be patient and silent, without anyone being able to tell if he was listening to the teacher or not, if any of it had a top and a bottom and sides for him or if it was nothing but a fog with orders Stand up Sit down Shut up Open the book to page . . . So and so sent to the office, orders one had to obey, because kids have to obey while waiting to become grown-ups.

Abel is a grown-up. He won't go to school any more. He's content. On his shoulder, a lunch bag with a mess tin with a snack and chocolate milk. He leaves whistling, we bought him some boots, the exact same ones he always wanted. It's still summer, working outside isn't uncomfortable. Abel always hated being kept indoors.

He brings home his first pay. An incredible pile of money. My mother takes all of it, and says what do you want me to buy you? You need a pair of pants, some shirts, you don't have anything left to wear. Abel only wants a pellet gun.

—What for! my mother exclaims in dismay. You're not going to shoot at birds anyway . . .

Abel, with excessive amazement, says that Of course not. Shoot at birds, is she crazy? He'll shoot at cans like at the fair But he'll do it by himself, he'll be able to shoot when he wants, as many times as he wants . . .

—No, says my mother It's dangerous. You're going to hurt someone.

Abel shuts up. Turns red. Starts to drool at the corners of his mouth. Okay, but only in the courtyard then, says my mother, and make really sure there's no one there Not your little sister not a cat not anything. You hear me?

—Yeah right, Ariane whispers to me, as if I would hang out back there! I'm not an idiot.

Until autumn, Abel is a man—a little man skinny as a reed, swimming in his boots, and his butt slipping off his very big bicycle—. Then Winter comes, and Abel cries. He freezes at the worksites The cinder blocks are frozen, tear at fingers that one can't feel any more The tools slip from hands Condensed breath blurs the vision Iron bars stick out everywhere twisted, rusted, trapping numb legs. The others make fun They say Drink a shot, apprentice, afterwards you'll feel better . . . I don't wanna go any more, says Abel. I've had enough, I don't wanna any more.

—How the fuck did I end up with such a little shit! bellows my father who falls silent just as quickly, as if surprised by his own intervention, and is consumed by the contemplation of his soup once again.

Him, he was on construction sites by the age of eleven. We all know it. We keep quiet. Besides, I go to high school, what do I have to complain about?

—Hey, my mother explains to Abel who is crying But your sister, she has a brain. While we . . . What do you want, my poor little one, if you'd learnt better in school you'd still be there too . . . But when you don't even have a junior-high degree, you've got to rely on your hands . . . Look at your father.

Abel doesn't look at anything or anyone. I look at my father who's eating his soup, the little veins in his temples swollen as if they were going to explode. Maybe it's nothing other than the sudden heat after the cold of the day, but maybe it's one of those amorphous bouts of temper without focus that surge on their own, not knowing very well whom to attack, and that ends up taking it out on the furnishings on the dishes on the window panes, on everything that can be pulverized instead of the elusive causes of injustice or absurdity.

—Work, says my mother, it's a little hard at the beginning, you have to get used to it. But after you've done it, you don't think about it any more, you'll see . . . And besides, that's life, what do you expect . . . Hey, look, I bought you gloves   They're fur-lined   Try them.

Abel cries a little longer, then grabs his gloves. He finds them pretty nice, puts his fingers in that are red Swollen   Cracked   Grey at the joints   The nails are broken, filthy. Blood underneath one of them. Just looking at his hands, you might think that Abel had had an accident. That only by the strength of his fingers was he able to extricate himself from a tunnel or an abyss that had collapsed on him. Because of his gloves, that fit him perfectly and smell of new leather, Abel begins to feel a bit happy again. He eats his soup, him too, before it gets too cold. And even though he eats without taking his gloves off, no one dares to point it out, not even Ariane who finished a long time ago and is chewing the inside of her cheeks.

Cut it out, my mother would say to Ariane when she caught her at it. Who's ever heard of having such a tic. There are some who chew their nails, but my daughter chews the skin of her cheeks, have you ever seen that? Stop chewing on yourself, idiot, you're going to bleed again. The more they grow the dumber they get, I swear.

—That's so true, Micheline would say sniffling up her snot mournfully, mine are the same. And to think that I was impatient for them to grow up.

—Eat a cookie instead, Margot would counsel Ariane. Are you bored?

—She's at that age when they don't really know what to do with themselves, Gertrude would say. We don't keep them busy enough, they get stupid . . .

—I'm thinking, Ariane would protest.

—You think too much, Gertrude would joke, I'm telling you. Look at Camille. At least she reads . . . What are you reading, my pretty?

—Someone's talkin' to you, says my mother.

I held up my book, so they could read the title, and I plunged back in without suspecting a thing. I had read so many books without alarming anyone, from the *Claudine* series that they took for sweet childishness, to *The Stranger*—title absolutely neutral —passing by *Jésus la Caille*, that probably sounded like a devotional book, *The Idiot* and *Dirty Hands* that the Mothers took for years to be something like a sequel to the Countess of Segur books . . . I had let my guard down.

At the same time as my mother, they all read the title. There was a moment's hesitation, that suddenly weighed on my reading. Silence on the part of the Mothers who, not being mine, don't allow themselves to comment, but are nonetheless watching to see what the author of my days is going to say in the face of this delicate situation.

I'm sure that without all those eyes watching to see what she'll do my mother would leave me the fuck alone, would let go that which is vaguely troubling her: after all I'm a big girl, I know a ton of stuff that she doesn't, and she systematically loses every argument with me by not even trying to build a case—My mother is logical, aware of her deficiencies, she has no excessive taste for Power and Discipline.—

But she's cornered by the gaze of her pals, above all those who have Principles like Micheline or Experience like Gertrude. So she has to say something, anything, that would prove that she's in command, otherwise they'll lecture her as soon as my back is turned You should You shouldn't Be careful Me if I were you Wha'd we tell you . . . I know them well enough that I want to bite them to bark at their calves to scatter them like hens to clear out a bare spot where my mother and I would be alone in our mutual tolerance.

But it's Ariane who explodes, she whom no one had rattled, except to tease her about her mordant thoughts, and who had taken the wise route of playing chequers with Abel who doesn't work on Saturday afternoons:

—It's surely a romance novel. 'Cheri', you say that alone, right? So what? She doesn't have the right to read a stupid romance novel at her age? And whaddya think we see at the movies? So we can't go to the movies any more, then? Anyway what's so terrible in love stories? Besides it's always the same thing, people who hold hands like kids, who kiss on the mouth, all that to end up in bed, and personally I don't see the big deal, but in the end all those stories that's all it is:

to always end up sleeping together after a whole load of shit . . . We know it Everyone knows it What are you looking at And then first of all . . .

—That's enough! says my mother to Ariane just at the moment when she had completely lost us all. You're wearing us out. Go out for some air, as a matter of fact it's not raining any more, that'll teach you to mind your own business. Git!

—Poor little sweetie, says Gertrude. Not only does she think, but on top of that she thinks out loud . . . That age is carefree . . .

Ariane goes out shrugging her shoulders.

—I'm going with you, Abel says hastily.

Abel flees arguments as some would flee a battlefield In distress, legs trembling, not knowing where to look, if he should run or duck for cover. The angry words that crisscross above his head, he watches them coming close as if they were lethal bullets. And if by bad luck one of the belligerents turns to him, expecting from him not even participation in the struggle or the explicit choice of a side, but only a point of view or an opinion, Abel goes gaga on the spot, as if physically stricken by disintegration, fissured under the gaze, all his facial features in disarray and let loose and leaking water from every hole: eyes, nostrils, corners of the mouth go all loose, not tightly sealed . . .

I don't know where that could come from, nor what liquefies him like that. Even when he was little, when my father and my mother were shouting, or just my father, Abel would tremble so much that he would piss himself standing up So much that in the end he would become as stiff as someone who had been electrocuted, the light of his eyes exploding inside his skull like the sparks of a blowtorch when one welds two pieces of iron together. In the end, he would fall, petrified, Ariane and I breaking the fall, accompanying him mechanically until he was horizontal, my mother shouting to God knows who 'He's gonna kill him!'

The little ones finally gone, the Mothers guffaw, except mine who still doesn't know if she should. Ariane's speeches always end up cheering everyone up, once the first shock is passed. Margot says It's true that she's grown . . . No doubt in the meantime she'd been feeling some remorse, in a sort of walk down memory lane towards her own extremely turbulent seventeen-year-old self. Even if things were different 'in those days', and if in the years since then she let herself get bitten by the bug for Education that transforms young crazy girls into respectable ladies. But to believe in their respectability, I would've had to not listen to their conversations.

—So? says Gertrude lighting one of her cigarettes that smell of caramel, so then you're dreaming of Prince Charming?

It was maybe an attempt at complicity, or a demonstration of an open mind, but several devils popped up in my head, as if spring-loaded.

—Aren't any Princes any more. And if there are any I leave them for whoever wants 'em.

—You're pretty generous, says Gertrude, but people say one thing . . .

She took on her look of knowing so much better, she who had 'lived', than a brat my age. And she insists:

—You say one thing, and then you knock around a bit . . . You'll do like your girlfriends, little vixen, but you gotta add a little style . . . . It's true that you put on eau de toilette, now, I've noticed it. Ha ha! But other than that . . .

—Oh, please! says my mother. Don't give her any more great ideas. She has plenty of time for some dipshit to mess around with her.

They all nodded vigorously   Oh yes! Oh right, I have plenty of time! My devils move, rile up my nerves. I say that I will not let myself be 'messed with', ME. Dead silence, where undecided shadows float. I hear my mother thinking this more strongly or more profoundly than the others   I hear her fear, unsettled, equivocal, almost brushing with its wing my past attempts at assassination from which she skips away with an almost perceptible jolt   I hear her bewilderment falling again flat as an oar, and derived from it: who is this girl, who came out of her belly, capable of 'everything', not resembling anything known and above all not her, the mother Who does she think she is claiming to be from another forest, of a different breed, and why not indeed I hear her smash herself against this unexpected wall This difference that I claim loud and clear, that negates her, her, as a model and as kin, and that even goes so far as to accuse her that accuses her, that judges her, that condemns her to a form of disdain . . . Oh! Mom, so much smaller than me and stumbling your way through life, shouting that someone's gonna kill your kid on you and incapable of defending him, I'm not putting you on trial but I don't want to end up like you 'cheering myself up' with a handful of poor girls who drivel on in the smoke and fumes of burnt coffee. I don't want to, that's all. I don't . . .

—Don't cry, says Margot. Look she's crying 'cause of your bullshit. It's nothing, my chickadee, have a cookie . . .

—It's true, Margot says again to Gertrude, you're not too cute with your jabs, ya don't even notice.

—But why're you crying? my mother says to me happily distracted from her drifting by this sudden manifestation of childishness, and ready to take out her handkerchief in case I didn't have one.

—Oh! says Gertrude always sententious even though she was bothered a little, she's at that age where you cry for no reason, come on . . . Read it, your *Chéri*, no one wants to take it from you, ain't that true, Odette?

—Evidently, says my mother who's troubled by these to-dos as much as me, I can tell, and who's vaguely mad at her pals for this whole comic interlude.

— . . . And then at least, says Gertrude, when you meet a handsome young man, you'll know right away what to call him.

They all laugh, except my mother who is still wondering over some things. Micheline says that in any case that's life, that kids grow up, that it's a perpetual starting over . . . She, when she met her guy, Larbi, listen to this . . .

I should have scrammed, like Ariane and Abel. But the devils hang on to me, their horns are out And then, in the nostalgic tenderness of Beginnings, Gertrude calls me as a witness—You'll see! One day you will bring a big handsome young man to your mother, that's it, that's life . . . —all those devils snickered together in the spray of sparks from their hooves:

—And why not a big beautiful young woman? If I wanted to?

I watch this stone sink, making endless concentric circles in the silence.

—Idiot! says my mother finally, in an attempt to shake off the shock. You think you're clever?

—It's just that crazy age, says Micheline, there's nothing to do . . .

—Ah, well! is all that Gertrude says lighting another cigarette. Well, well . . .

Her sombre gaze literally jumped to my face, abruptly wiped clear of that laughing softness that cloaked her in affability. I should have been suspicious of her, who had 'lived' so much. Now she looks me over woman to woman, as though testing in my eyes the consistency of that joke, its exact percentage of sincerity and of provocation.

I will not flinch. I didn't flinch.

—Pay no attention, says my mother, you can see clearly that she'll say anything to make herself seem interesting. Micheline is right, it's a crazy age.

Gertrude's gaze pulls back from me undecided.

—What time is it? worries my mother who would really like to escape this machine set in motion who knows how and which in her opinion bodes nothing good.

—Four thirty, says Margot, you have time. You want some joe?

—Me, says Gertrude trying to blow smoke rings, I lived with a woman when I was young . . .

The Mothers jump.

—You? says Micheline pushing away Margot's coffee pot: no thanks, it's burnt-to-hell, your joe. Is this a joke?

—No no, says Gertrude. No joke. It was hell-on-earth, that's all there is to say: hell-on-earth!

—Did she hit you? worries Margot.

General laughter: considering Gertrude's size, even subtracting the kilos put on since then, it's insane to imagine that another woman could ever clean her clock, even for a man it would be rather risky. The Mothers wallow even more in their fit of giggles since they don't know how to sneak off before Gertrude unloads her unexpected and sulfurous 'experience' that disturbs us all like a commando unit of mosquitos bursting in through the window. My mother scratches her shoulder, starts to talk about my homework. I say calmly that it's done. Too bad for her. An environment . . . says Gertrude, oh my children! She looks at the ashtray as if it had begun to swarm with cockroaches or some other dirty pests. And to me, with a cautionary effort:

—One day, I'll tell you . . .

—How dare you! my mother suddenly balks. You're not gonna tell her anything at all. Just because she let out some wiseass comment, you're not going to give her the details of your . . . Well, anyway.

—That's right, Gertrude admits with a look that's just as dark and heavy and hangdog in my direction, I'm talking nonsense.

Just to unwind my mother from whatever is keeping her tied to her chair, I suddenly remember a translation exercise that needs revising.

—Ah, sighs my mother as if I gave her back her oxygen, you see, when you think hard . . . Let's go, go call your brother and your sister and go home quick, I'm coming.

I say goodbye politely to everyone, including Gertrude whose gaze seeks out mine with a sudden insistence that repulses me. But I stand up to it, hoping that she could read in mine the degree to which I'm indifferent to her nasty self. How little it concerns me. And how much my life is new and solid and without any dubious swarming. After all, you have the dirty critters that you deserve, it's a matter of perspective. But when Gertrude smiles at me, with that sort of sadness she has for looking far off in the distance, I understand that I'm fooling myself: her gaze is not hostile, nor even disapproving, and suddenly I slide out of control. It's—curiously—her gaze of the Black Forest The look that calls and supplicates and maybe even holds itself back just before the jump. That one which in pulling back chills my body, without me being able to determine if I was abandoned or saved.

In any case uncertainty was—will remain?—my natural state. Or, if it's not uncertainty, at least ambiguity, so often there are almost always a minimum of two possible interpretations of the least fact word or look. And if my future career forces me to total objectivity, it shows me at that same time that total objectivity doesn't exist, and that the truth is in itself a brittle and uncertain matter. In the end, and in the hope of exactitude, I organize my memories in the conditional.

If love is really abduction, that instantaneous removal from all that had been until then one's natural milieu, that shifting upside down into a parallel universe not necessarily habitable but of a sumptuous harmony, then yes, I was in love with Clara.

But who, I? Because I had been pulverized crossing the finish line Because my debris in suspension reorganized itself according to other laws or accidents Because I had become SOMEONE ELSE before having had time to determine WHO I had been at first (if in any case I had even had a proper existence, if I hadn't settled for being the meeting point of untethered forces) or who I could have been without this sort of accident, this mental pile-up . . .

While waiting for all that to resolve itself and to be able to function one way or another, I sleep. I sleep a great deal. I have bloody dreams, I'm moving cadavers, hiding them, drowning them, and always erasing the traces—not so much to avoid suspicion or punishment but rather to reconstruct a sort of innocence for myself in my own eyes.—But these are unwilling cadavers, they float back up to the surface of the waters spill out of suitcases fall from closets pop out of carpets where they've been rolled up, with the tranquil obstinacy of heavy, inert, motionless things. I sweat. I'm exhausted. I sleep more than ever. It's without beginning nor end, and without an apparent solution.

Thursdays, I go see Clara. She's just bought a scooter—a pretty little pearl-grey machine with flashy chrome-work which she zooms around on, her hair all flying behind her in the wind.—From the saddlebag the handle of a tennis racket pokes out.

—Would you like to learn to play? asks Clara.

But at the last moment, I balk at the ridiculous little mini-skirt that you have to wear. I settle for watching Clara run, miss balls with elegance, and finally give up, panting with much grace.

Beaten to a pulp, asserts Clara. It's been too long since I last played. You should have played with me, maybe I would've had a chance . . . Ugh! I'm beat.

The beads of sweat run all over her, even from her hair. I wrap her in a towel I smooth her I dry her I would lick her if I could. Oh! Clara even her sweat was attractive and unsettling . . . People like that never smell bad, never You'd think that each pore right down to the root of each hair is scoured purified scented until it secretes only clear water with the scent of an overheated plant.

—What are you thinking about, Camille?

—Nothing.

—You're really easy to get along with, said Clara smiling at me while taking the towel back from me to sponge herself off more energetically. Unless you're being particularly, uh . . . Cautious . . . Shall we go back?

I have a house on the cliff, Clara had said to me. It belongs to me—the house, of course, not the cliff—Jean-Jacques doesn't like the countryside, we almost never set foot there. Would you like it if I took you there?

It's my father who built it, Clara was saying. My father was an avant-garde architect, he worked a lot with the Americans . . . Jean-Jacques doesn't like Americans Nor modern architecture He didn't like my father either I wonder if he likes anything or anyone . . . Then she falls silent, noticing maybe that I have shrunk considerably inside my skin, inhibited like a kid between the dentist and the architect, me who is nothing at all wrapped in my duffel coat that falls off sideways.

—What are you thinking about? says Clara, with that attentive smile in whose light I suddenly lose all my dullness. Hmmm? speak up!

—Why did you marry him?

—For love, says Clara brushing my bangs brusquely out of my eyes. One always marries for love, didn't you know that? Even if it's for love of contradiction. C'mon, get on the bike! We're going to hunt spiders, that'll give us some exercise. And hold me tight.

I close my arms on Clara's waist like on the neck of a fabled horse, Pegasus or a unicorn or some other creature too beautiful to exist in real life I'm soldered to the leather of her jacket To the body that I feel underneath To her warmth like that of a sun-soaked animal To her scent of exotic grasses that grow at the other end of the earth. Her black curls lifted by the wind beat me on the forehead like a mane.

The house is backed up to a niche in the plateau, turned toward a sea that can barely be glimpsed on the horizon, a thin grey line under the grey of the sky. Everywhere the cries of seagulls. Everywhere the immense sky. The short grass of the plateau . . . The sensation not that the wind slides over you, but that one is sliding in the wind, as though insidiously blown towards the drop-off.

—Breathe, Clara said unbuttoning her jacket.

And then as if this explained that:

—Here, this is my home.

She was saying it humbly, as if she expected some sort of forgiveness or complicity from me, something in any case that would be a sharing, a thing in common, even unspoken, and that would keep us together. But I didn't dare speak to her any more. Still less did I dare touch her. Walking in the wind we were carving out two parallel furrows that the grass slowly filled back up.

You have all the luck, Ariane comments. And why didn't you want to play tennis? That must be fun, tennis . . . And why didn't you bring me with you to that joint, up there, not even once?

I remind her with a certain impatience that there are only two seats on a scooter.

Obviously, says Ariane in that enigmatic tone that seems to uncover devious subtexts beneath my most anodyne words, obviously obviously . . . So she likes you?

I say that I don't know, shit, and after all that's not the question.

—But what is, then, the question? Ariane insists barely missing the windowpane with one of her damn balls. Seriously I'm asking you. If it were me, it would bug me not to know. Me, I'd bust up everything I'd fucking set the curtains on fire I . . . Aw shit!

It's one of two things, concludes Ariane: either you have a shitload of patience or you're scared shitless. You poor thing.

But between us, Ariane goes on in a smooth, level voice that's all the more menacing, you could talk to me, from time to time, before I drag it out of you. If only just to, I dunno . . . To distract yourself. Right? I still exist, Ariane was saying, even when you don't notice.

In order to shut Ariane up, to neutralize this vertiginous whirlwind of words that strips the inside of my skull, I tell her about this house of glass of stone of concrete   The heavy rolling shutters that blinker it like blindfolds   That Clara pushes, with such pathetic effort that I'm obliged to help her push   That creak. I say they need oiling. I tell about the immense skylights   The whole sky entering into the house   The three little living rooms, and how one passes from one to the other by going up or going down a few steps   Yes, that's it, no doors or walls: just simple differences of level, and so you have one big room and at the same time these completely distinct nooks   The library nook   The living-room nook   The fireplace nook . . .

—A fireplace! exclaims Ariane who hadn't interrupted me yet but who's suddenly made impatient by the vagueness of my descriptions. Is it big?

—Rather, yes.

—How big?

—This big.

—You could burn a tree trunk in it?

—Uh . . . Half of one, yes. A big one.

—How big?

—Like this.

Ariane admires the diameter of the tree, all the while chewing the inside of her cheek.

—Stop gnawing on yourself.

—What else, says Ariane.

I tell about the kitchen-laboratory The breakfast nook whose small balcony gives out onto the immense living room with the skylights And all the bedrooms which you get to by way of another little balcony also looking out over . . . and each one with its own bathroom twice as big as ours, each in a different colour with a sink and tub matching the tile on the walls . . .

—A bathroom for each bedroom, says Ariane suddenly suspicious, you're laying it on a bit thick, right?

—I swear I'm not. But the most beautiful . . .

—What, what's the most beautiful? Ariane presses me tormented by my hesitations and visibly holding herself back from shaking me to extract from me some really beautiful images in place of this colourless mush that I'm trying to tell her, so, what is it?

—It's the piece of the cliff that comes into the living room.

—Stop fucking with me, says Ariane, or I'm going to knock your block off. Ya think I'm a moron!

I explain to Ariane that this is a house integrated into the environment The kind that you don't really see except in America or in movies I swear I'm telling you that the cliff comes into one of the little living rooms A big chunk stripped down, all clean, in a corner It looks like a rock at low tide And when it rains the water runs on it in little cascades, gets drained out under the floor by a special system . . . And if you don't believe me, too bad.

—I believe you, says Ariane after a moment of reflection. And she repeats, as though vaguely blown away I believe you I believe you . . . Did you light a fire, at least?

I say no, it's spring, or had Ariane forgotten.

—So what? says Ariane. A spring this rotten . . . And a house never lived in . . . It wouldn't have hurt anyone.

The common sense of my little sister Ariane flattens me with its coarse clarity. Neither of us thought of it. And besides it wasn't warm in the house on the cliff. Clara had zipped up her jacket, foraging in the kitchen in search of something to make me to drink. She had ended up finding a little tea dust in a tin, and some bits of sugar in another. No lemon, obviously, and the tea spoons couldn't be found.

—Drink, said Clara stirring her tea with a knife handle, next time will be better We're going to get organized It's pretty nasty, no? But at least it's hot. Drink, Camille, you look frozen stiff . . . She made a move as though to touch my cheek—or maybe my bare neck—but she stopped abruptly. She would never touch me, except my shoulders to steer me in the right direction when walking, or to kiss me hello or goodbye. But in the cold of that empty house, her gaze closed around me like a sort of protection or as if waiting for some stumble, she said that I could address her using *tu*, she had told me to often enough.

As we were leaving, after another round of pushing shutters and locks that work badly, Clara proposed:

—You want to drive? It's simple, watch.

I watch, but I refuse: today, my hands are frozen. Nestled against Clara's back, her hair whipping my forehead, I shut my eyes on crazy images scattered bit by bit by the wind. On the walls, there were real paintings More beautiful than I could ever have believed could exist.

—You like painting?

I didn't know. It was the first time that I saw real paintings, and not just photographs. I'll have to take you to the museums, Clara had said I'll have to . . . I'll have to . . . The wind howls in my ears I have my cheek on the leather of the jacket that slowly grows warm Between my arms, I feel Clara's torso breathing And I imagine the obstacle and the accident and me soldered to her forever, all flesh forever mixed together Dissolved into one another Inseparable.

So, the day of my defiance of the Mothers, I ran to see Clara, after pretending to hit on this sudden idea to which I had already applied the maximum of my ingenuity.

—Where are you going at this time of day? said my mother.

—I need some information. I'm going to see Clara.

—Listen, said my mother, I don't like you to go bothering that woman for every little thing. After all, she . . .

After all, nothing. Everybody pisses me off. And if that's the first time that I let myself slam the door of the house, I doubt it will be the last And if they don't like it . . . then it's very simple: I'll break it all to bits I am angry enraged worked up in a furore

There's a whole troop of demons galloping alongside me Shouting that this has gone on long enough That I am coming completely undone That I want someone to kill me now or to welcome me in That

—Do you get it?

So, I can use *tu* with you As a guarantee of friendship, right Well, let's use *tu* It's now or never Even if the term 'friendship' masks all sorts of possible ambiguities while I love precision, me We will be precise later This will become clear on its own Clara, with her habitual sweetness which I was beginning to suspect was nothing other than knowing how to put others off, could not evade the issue eternally by laughing—which also prevented me from getting angry—What do I mean by that? But . . . Oh! Camille, you're merciless with your demands for definition. Believe me, friendship between two people can be felt and HAPPENS. It doesn't define itself. Don't we get along well together? Yes. Exactly. I'm running, the devils on my heels, the knife in my teeth, and a bomb in each hand. Now or never:

—Do you get it?

Clara's sombre gaze, at first resting on mine with the same quivering attention to all my states of being, seems to slip from me like a cloth that is a little too light. One of those that won't hold off the wind.

I try to catch her gaze again by seizing her by the shoulders:

—You've got nothing to say?

I'd never touched her before, except on the scooter through her jacket. The shape of her shoulders under the thin fabric of her dress, their heat, their proximity upset me even more. Then I perceive their imperceptible retraction, as if they were melting on the spot, they too were slipping away in a reflex of evasion or at least of prudent withdrawal from the imposed contact, that one wished neither to push away nor to put up with . . . In the end she escaped from me, with a turning movement officially reserved for manoeuvring away from any interrupter who couldn't wait their turn:

—Yes I do, I have something to say. Of course, I do. But really . . . Listen, Camille, you're still so young . . . All these questions can be put off until later, don't you think so?

—No.

Listen, said Clara her large sombre gaze set before me like a screen or a mirror or something closed in any case, and her vanished smile was replaced by a very light withdrawal of her lower lip Listen, I'm sorry, I'm not able to answer you. I don't know.

Then I said something stupid: that I would come back when she did know. Which made her smile, with a curious mix of amusement and sorrow.

Afterwards I'm hunkered down in my bed. My two fists on my eyes to push back down these images that are henceforth dead or should be considered as such Clara standing in front of me in the dentist's waiting room Oh, are you there? Come in, we'll chat for five minutes. Clara asking me for news of my little sister Ariane—Does she still play with marbles? Again and again I watch her large black eyes, surprised, that look away That come back to take up my gaze as if there were nowhere else in the room towards which they might direct themselves for long. Others always say to me Why do you look at me like that? Clara says nothing, ever. She hands me things, books, as if to draw my attention elsewhere Have you read? Have you noticed? I had or had not read. I had always noticed. A sort of fugitive despair spreads on her face that seems naked, suddenly, without defence, as though on the brink of coming undone. Then I want to confess the theft of the flower but I still don't dare. Clara turned towards me again while I mount the scooter, and smiling at me on the fly. Clara standing in the wind of the cliff, and gliding lightly in her furrow of crushed grass that goes parallel to mine Clara wrapped in her jacket to feel less cold, and her gaze around me like a guard or a suspicion, who knows, and who says All the same, what if you use *tu* with me finally, it's about time?

It's fucked up. It's too late. I'll ask Ariane to go return her books to her, or else I'll leave them with the secretary. And if only the end of the world would bury all of us, Abel Ariane and me and this stinking little street and Margot's dump and all the disaster zones on earth and the houses for the sub-humans where there aren't even toilets and all the dizzying books and all that hasn't yet had time to be recognized and classified inside my head opened up by accident and there's nothing left but chaos scrap metal and blood mixed together and guts exposed to the open air because I'm spurting from everywhere and I'm crushed dead.

It's another day, but I don't know which one any more. Coming suddenly mentally unhinged, I go up Gertrude's stairs. For once it's really truly spring The day is luminous and warm, and I climb in the darkness because I couldn't locate the switch The walls that I'm hugging so as not to trip echo with the sound of the blood in the palm of my hands It's the beginning of the afternoon Gertrude is sleeping, I'm going to get yelled at Groping the walls Going up I'm gonna wake her up Don't trip Hold onto the wall Go up What am I going to say to her Go up some more Go on I'd never gone inside Gertrude's, ever, I'd just gone to knock once just to ask for salt but I stayed on the landing What am I going to be able to say to her That my watch had stopped That I lost track of time Completely idiotic That I want to see Mylene, why not But to do what And then Mylene isn't there, in any case, she works, everyone knows that I will have forgotten She'll see clearly that I'm . . . We'll see, shit! Go on I'm so thirsty I'll tell her I'm thirsty, whatever.

What the hell are you doing there? said Gertrude closing her peignoir with a sleepy gesture. What do you want? Did something happen?

The somewhat oriental curtains smell of dust, filter the day, vaguely break up the light. I mumble Mylene's name—Are you nuts, or what? says Gertrude in her drawling voice while closing the door behind me She's been working for the past three weeks, Mylene, that ain't it, right? And what do you want with her?

I scuff the floor with the tip of my soles, in an effort to hold myself almost upright, to not sink into the shininess of the peignoir, at least not right away to not fall completely silent to ask for a glass of water to explain anything at all That I had lent Mylene . . . which I now urgently need . . .

—Eh? What?

Gertrude found a cigarette—one of her caramel cigarettes—and a brush, that she passes slowly through her hair. You seen the time? No, it's that . . .

watch stopped . . . I'm stammering in such a pathetic way that Gertrude looks at me more attentively. A beam of light briefly explodes in the glass of water and disperses itself there—Drink, that'll make it better. Crunch of the brush in the black mane where there shine threads of silver with a sudden flash. This is an old woman. Older than my mother.—What do you want, besides the water? Huh?

The silky leaf-pattern of the peignoir transports the gaze in imperceptible slippages gyrations layerings. Gertrude's teeth, still beautiful, in the light The fire in the ring on her finger Between her eyelids suddenly immobile At the end of the cigarette that she crushes in the ashtray after having just taken only three puffs. A sneaky drifting of my train of thought leaves me paralysed Vacant Nauseated The whole room around me throbbing with muted lights Christmas-tree lights in a dark room The shine of a razor in a ray of daylight Minuscule sparkling of crystals on the edge of the abyss . . . What do you want? insists Gertrude as if I hadn't already (or not really) answered, her voice strangely muffled and continuing to vibrate in the air after she stopped speaking.

The darkness of her eyes is on me An oppressive darkness and seemingly just at its breaking point That will unfurl spread itself block the exits . . . She looks brutally at my throat, at my mouth, and I feel as though I'm being swallowed Emptied Turned inside out like a glove by the inside of my body . . .

—Get the fuck out of here, murmured Gertrude with a sort of surly tenderness and as if she were holding herself back from coming towards me. Go on, get. Go. No fuss. Fuck off home to your mother.

I found myself in the darkened staircase like a night where I was forced to wander without end. I forget how long I stayed there, befuddled not suffering from anything any more, listening to my fear and the vague regret in my stomach die down.

Once I was finally able to get out again into the sun—that dusty sun of our town, always vaguely stinking of the smells of sewers and of the gutter—I had the brief and nauseous impression of meeting myself without recognizing myself. Sensation of a 'me' eternally fictive, eternally foiled, wandering without purpose one step ahead of some anathema . . .

—Where'd you come from? Ariane asked simply, crouched on the sidewalk, barely turning her head in my direction. Huh? Look.

She was still teasing a bug, with the end of a twig: Look, it's pretty.

Ariane fiddles with insects with indifference, curiosity or sympathy, maybe, eternally surprised by the horror that I feel about it. She always tries to appeal to my good faith, to my objectivity:

—C'mon look. It isn't mean. Isn't it beautiful?

I say If you say so, yes. But to me it's disgusting.

This time, it was a blue beetle. Light blue, electric.

—Exactly the shade of Abel's eyes, says Ariane whose gaze leaps to my face like a diabolical spark. Aren't they pretty, Abel's eyes?

She turned the beetle over on its back, for laughs. To play. To scare it. Generally, she put the little creatures back on their legs quickly, in the spirit of order or justice, you can't really tell.

Yes. Of course, Abel's eyes are beautiful. I don't know why this remark seemed etched with danger to me. I can't take my eyes off the wriggling beetle, off the black articulated armour of its belly, off the flurrying of its legs—way too many legs for an insect who flies—that upsets my stomach with an idiotic panic that is resistant to all reasoning, with an uncontrollable revulsion:

—Did you see the underside? Well LOOK then, you look too. It's horrid. It gives me the creeps. What do you want me to do? Let it be.

—Are you afraid? Ariane asked again standing straight before the overturned beetle which is still contorting itself in vain. My big sister Camille is afraid of a little beetle. My big sister Camille is scared shitless . . .

—Oh well! Ariane sighed with a strange tone of indulgence. Let's go, c'mon!

And with a brisk strike of her heel, she crushed the bug. Reduced it to black debris cut through with sparks of sky and still twitching imperceptibly. These fragments smashed into one another, bent, chewed, shredded and still moving feebly, cause me to be hit with nausea for real. I want to slap Ariane.

—So why'd you do that?

—You were afraid, Ariane said in her hard voice, hammering, implacable. You need to know what you want.

And with that she finished off the beetle by grinding it into the dust with strikes of her heel, face closed, as if she were angrily fulfilling some unsavoury task that had been imposed on her.

Abel has his BB gun. As promised, he doesn't hunt. The only game he ever fires on, besides the nylon feathers at the fair, is a pile of small cardboard targets that he pins on the wall of the cellar and whose concentric circles are equally riddled with holes. The cellar wall being otherwise almost entirely riddled with pellets, you can't tell if Abel is or isn't a good shot.

Sometimes, he walks in the neighbourhood, the gun hanging from his shoulder, wearing his sage green rubber boots, and a waxed hat like fishermen wear, the same colour as the boots.

Marie-who-has-two-sexes calls him the 'explorer'. She stops pushing her broom in the gutter to watch him pass. She still has the same straight grey hair, brush-cut like those old paratroopers, and her light eyes, a little dead and seemingly endlessly perplexed. She doesn't nod her head hello Doesn't lift her chin in greeting like my mother's friends She just says with her voice ringing like an empty barrel Hello, Explorer! And Abel responds Hello, Marie, and he passes And after a moment of reflection Marie-who-has-two-sexes takes up her stiff-bristled broom again and clears her gutter again because that's what the good Lord put her on earth for on one of his indecipherable Paths.

But despite the fur-lined gloves, the boots and the gun on Sundays, we wonder if Abel still wants to play at being a man.

Abel doesn't wash himself any more doesn't fix his hair any more doesn't shave any more. Even his voice has become clammy and heavy and sticky. Seated with his back rounded and his elbows on the table and scratching his greasy locks of otherwise flat and dull hair, he reads the same books over and over, books that are thoroughly interchangeable, splattered with blood on the cover, where women get their necks wrung like poultry.—Ever since he's had some money in his pocket, that's all he buys, except for candies that he shares with Ariane. His nails are growing flat and hard, each underlined with a black crescent. A light beard, with a strange, pimply look, eats away at his cheeks like a diseased rash. Go shave, says my mother. Have you looked at yourself in a mirror? To think I used to have the handsomest little boy in the neighbourhood . . .

In the street they say That kid's getting weirder and weirder. When he goes by, they hide the girls who might still be possible prey. Abel doesn't notice anything or anyone. He's alone in the world behind his electric blue eyes, like in a charred landscape. They say to my mother Listen, Odette, between you and me, your son . . . Me, if I were you . . . Are you sure at least that he isn't dangerous or that he won't be someday? . . .

In the end my mother said, in a voice that died out a little as if a blade was going through her throat, that Abel was harmless, the poor kid And that all that was nothing but twisted gossip. Since then, she's angry with half the ladies of the street, and us with their bitch daughters, except of course Mylene who's been working the past few months in the same factory as Gertrude and who never hangs out in the streets on Sundays, because now she's too big and in any case she's tired.

Sometimes, when I'm at Margot's, more or less reading and more or less listening to the chitchat of the Mothers, I have the impression of looking through another slitted window. Then I start to have a sort of very vague urge to vomit, like you get on carousels, on the down swings.

To the theatre of shadows that rise up inside and fade away, in a light so faint that you wonder if you can suddenly see in the dark, answers another theatre, radically opposed and symmetrical: an outdoor theatre without the slightest bit of shade, with the ruckus of conversations the odour of coffee that boils and reboils the bodies hunched on the edges of chairs and Micheline's knitting on which it eternally rains drops of snot. Unity of place: Margot's kitchen. Unity of time: the same afternoon begins again over and over. Unity of action: the standstill of the Mothers' lives. Lives barely distinct from one another, snarled in the same skein, from which they pull this or that thread depending on the weather what the newspaper says or who they ran into that day.

A dark place, with its harrowing fascination, a light place, where you can watch them grow old and drivel on about the misery of the world. Where to put yourself? And where am I then, since I'm not inside nor outside, alternately watching from each side as though through a crack?

—I can see your ass, Abel had said with this new, wet, heavy voice that stuck to your skin.

—So what? said my little sister Ariane, struck as though all her nerves had just been lit up all at once by the same jolt. So? Does it turn you on?

Without thinking, without even clearly seeing how she suddenly hardened on all sides became a little rock a wall of granite a pebble hurtling down into an abyss, I slapped Ariane:

—How many times have you been told not to squirm like that all the time? It's true, after all. It's like you have ants in your pants.

Bitch! caterwauled Ariane through her teeth which were still a bit too big for her little mouth Bitch Bitch Bitch Ariane was still saying with tears in her eyes as hard as marbles Touch me again and you'll see If you do that again I'll demolish you I'll walk all over you I'll tear your guts out Bitch bitch bitch Ariane was still saying while gnawing on her pillow much later in our room No but what a bitch seriously what . . . She didn't stop until the pillow was completely soaked, the pillowcase reduced to shreds out of which the ends of feathers poked like nails.

Then I was able to take my hands out of my pockets and gather up what remained of my little sister Ariane Without trying to make her see reason Without bothering to distinguish between her head and her knees. I cradled against me the mass of her hair her nails her teeth her bones sticking out under her skin, until the whole thing calms itself and pulls itself together and sighs, in the choppy rhythm of a sob: You . . . You never had, you, ants in your pants?

In the doorway, there were Abel's eyes Like two holes of fire in his skull. I said I'm warning you, if you tell even one little bit of this to Mom you won't come out of it alive.

—I didn't do anything . . . protested Abel who was already distraught. I said no. That no one had done anything. So that's why there was nothing to tell.

—Ariane ate her pillow, said Abel all the same.

—It's because she has a toothache.

Abel meditated on that explanation without saying anything, his gaze on his feet. Then he asked humbly if he could come in. Then I took both of them bowling.

You never know how much Abel understands, what part he loses or unravels, while he drags his boots in the dust with that air he has of being nowhere, of never recognizing anything, of wandering between endless walls without ever finding a door.

The spring, that year, was still. Sticky like wet ashes. Eternal like a gigantic ruin. And every day the same litanies were repeated Abel, go shave, you look like a thief. Abel, you hear me? Go . . .

Abel's back doesn't budge His fingers slowly scratch his hair, there his nails collect their grease. Except for the slow scratching of his nails, Abel is completely immobile, hunched over his book.

Ariane crosses the room, juggling with her little balls

—You'll hit the lamp with one of those, says my mother. Good God, are all my kids idiots?

—Then Ariane palms all her balls in a single hand and contemplates Abel's back.

—Abel, you hear what I'm saying to you? repeats my mother whose voice begins imperceptibly to strain itself. Go shave. And while you're at it wash that lousy hair. Or I'll shave it off.

Abel still hasn't budged. His immobile, round-shouldered back seemed to swell, to fill up the room. Pouring off him it's like there are vibrations of a hostility so intense that Ariane and me we don't dare even look at each other again.

With an exasperated gesture, my mother sent the book flying. The unhinged cover soars heavily like a big black bird spotted with red, slams into my forehead, and finally falls at my feet. Then Ariane pulls me back, as if there were still time to protect me from something Meanwhile Abel finally unfolds himself, his eyes like two light holes between his beard and his hair, heavy, and as if they contained a scream situated somewhere above or below the range of sound.

My mother sighs and lets her shoulders fall, as if she'd just lifted an extraordinary weight. Ariane begins to whistle. And me I'm watching the first flies of the season take flight, with the sudden urge to get away from everything, to a place where nothing would ever stick to my skin, if it exists A sort of absolute death without burial nor cadaver A disappearance as radical as if I had never existed A fractious refusal to have been born, there you go. It wasn't worth it It wasn't fair Something was rigged from the beginning and this shapeless world doesn't interest me, where Clara let me stupidly leave and doesn't call me back.

—Don't sweat it, says to me Ariane who detects all my breakdowns, even minimal ones. Don't sweat it, doll, one day we'll leave for another country With a real sun With avenues planted with trees With, I dunno, like, lots of people dancing and singing. You'll see.

While waiting, I didn't dare ask her to go in my place to return Clara's books—God knows what commentary she would've been capable of adding.—Since sending them in the mail or bringing them back to the secretary would've been even more stupid, I went there myself, at the end of several weeks.

—There. I ought to have brought them back to YOU right away, Madame. In any case, I didn't read them.

—Why? said Clara, as if she had forgotten.

—Because. Because I have to study for the bac.

—That's right, said Clara whose smile came back, unsinkable and almost joyous. But why are YOU bringing them back to me, then, you dummy?

She had grabbed me by my collar:—Come on in, we have things to discuss. I suppose you can stop 'studying' for half an hour?

Clara. Clara I love you. Clara I'm at your feet You can walk on me cut the skin from my belly and from my wrists You can drown me burn me spear me twist me grate my skin and my nerves smash me into walls and scatter me in a fine powder . . . But not kiss me lightly as though I'd just left you yesterday, with the same smile as usual Not offer me tea with lemon while jostling me affectionately like one who was naughty and who's pardoned Not that. Not this adult rigmarole. Not this odious counterfeit of affection that would've been out of place, that one would need to set to one side or the other, and wait wait we'll find . . .

—No. I don't want tea. I love you. Take it or leave it.

—I know, said Clara, without a smile this time. I'm not a complete idiot. It's not worth smashing everything over. But me I don't . . . Well, you understand, I'm married . . .

I like you a lot, said Clara gravely, and that leaves me . . . pretty embarrassed. Do you really think that it's that serious?

Then she lifted her eyes, her large sombre gaze covering me with a peace that was sort of hesitant, as though watchful, her irrepressible smile coming back to her lips in impalpable shivers:

—I don't really know what to do, Camille . . . I . . . I didn't want this to happen. I don't want this to be a drama. I'm your friend. Only your friend . . . You understand? No? You really don't want some tea? . . .

It's crazy how much I was able to work, in the weeks that followed. Work and sleep. Sleep. While the situation slowly got bogged down, Clara acted exactly as if nothing had changed. As if I'd said nothing As if she didn't know all my feelings Or rather, as if the fact of having identified and admitted them once and for all had exorcised them Chased them far from us Engulfed in a sort of purgatory-time from which sooner or later they would emerge modified cooled down weakened inoffensive Finally conforming to the norms required for an appropriate relationship. As if it would suffice to let them soak in a bath of patience for them to lose their harshness and slowly fade . . .

I often woke up on the last image of an atrocious or sinister or gloomy dream: undefined creature howling like an animal, mouth wide open over its cut tongue. Or else endless rows of streets with completely grey walls without windows or doors. Or, again and always, the little man in black to whom I speak with a servile animation and who never listens to me.

—It's curious, Clara had said. Listen:

'Next to me came to sit
A stranger dressed in black
Who looked like a brother to me.'

I said that I knew the verse, yes. But this one didn't look like me at all, and was surely not my brother.

Until the first days of summer, Clara didn't mention her house on the cliff again. But on a radiant Wednesday that tore up the grey like a miracle, she came to get me at school, let me drive the scooter, yelling to me in the wind that smelt of new leaves and rain water that was in the process of drying:

—If we go up there tonight, would your parents . . .

—What?

—We could do some housekeeping . . . And then tomorrow we could get up really early, we'd have a whole day . . .

—What are you saying?

— . . . It's beautiful outside. BEAUTIFUL . . . What do you think of that?

Well, said my mother, as for what I think of it . . . You understand, those people and us, we're not from the same world . . . But since she's your friend . . . Listen, doll, you do what you want, I don't know. Sleep over, why not. Maybe she's bored, that woman . . . Go find out. And besides she's attached to you because you're smarter than the people from around here, that makes sense . . .

Me, my mother was saying, I'd be happy to invite her here, given all the time you spend at her place, it'd be more appropriate. But . . . But I'm afraid of not having much to say . . . Okay. Okay. You know best.

On route to the cliff, I'm driving the scooter again. The dentist has left, after having grumbled something vague about that shack that they ought to think about selling, finally. Before it falls apart. Clara didn't say anything. At least not in front of me. I can't figure out if he knew or not that I was part of the expedition.

I have Clara's arms around my torso, her belly and her chest clinging to my back. Since it's a little cold with the setting of the sun, I feel the hardening of her nipples through the wool of our sweaters. And if I go a little too fast, she pulls me back on the straight and narrow with a very light pressing of her fingers against my flanks.

If I were to die like this, exploded in the midst of the sunset in the midst of this giddiness in full delirium, I believe I would be satisfied with my life. All the same, I slow down, because Clara's very reasonable fingers ask me to. And I think that Ariane is right to shower me with her scorn after all.

Afterwards, while Clara empties the saddlebags literally crammed with provisions, I gather stuff to make a fire to warm up this icebox a little. There's some very dry wood in a shed, just waiting for us. It must be at least five years' old, says Clara helping me break up the twigs.

—You're sure it isn't seven?

—Huh? Why? No . . . I don't think so. No. No, not as many as that. I also turned on all the radiators, it'll be faster and more efficient. Why seven years?

—I would've preferred seven.

—We've got to put more on, says Clara, or else it'll make a measly flame that'll go out right away . . .

—Why seven exactly? No, not like that. Have you ever lit a fire?

—Never. Because in stories, it's always at the end of seven years that something happens.

—What things? says Clara foolishly.

Then she shuts up, and teaches me how to light a fire. There. With only one match.

—Why don't you ever come here?

—I told you, says Clara. Jean-Jacques hates the countryside. This house. This place.

—But on vacation, with friends . . . His friends . . . Or colleagues, I don't know . . .

I don't like my husband's colleagues, says Clara. They're morons. I don't like my family's friends either, Clara says then after a slight hesitation.

—Morons too?

—Not all of them, smiles Clara, happily. But I don't like their politics.

As for my own friends, Clara says then gazing fixedly at the fire, those from the past . . . They've scattered to the four corners of the earth . . . They come back from time to time. Not often. Never for long. We barely know each other any more. So, there. This house has almost always been empty, since the beginning . . .

And it doesn't suit it, says Clara with a gesture of sadness or of excuse. Don't you think so?

I contemplate all this space which is indeed lifeless, where it was peaceful like in a church   Where one wouldn't even dare to shout. On the piece of the cliff, thin sparkling streams recall that it rained all the last few days.

I say that I saw something like that in a film. It was *Tristan and Isolde*, I think. A stream went through a room. One day, it carried a love letter . . .

Clara smiles, as though randomly. Then she spoke too loudly, while almost extinguishing the kindling fire under a thick log. She says that so far that one hasn't really caught fire.

I say that she's going to kill the fire. That she surely hadn't looked hard enough, and she turned her eyes away, as if she feared, looking at that instant, that she might see.

She says   Mind your own business, that she still knows how to build a fire, that I shall see what I shall see . . .

I say that it's not a letter that she needs, but at least a cruise ship, in her stream. And then I say nothing more at all, so much has Clara fully disappeared behind she who is arranging the logs Who arranges the logs The logs And so much my own existence has become to me suddenly an object of perplexity and of doubt.

—I'm thirsty, Clara finally says with as much effort as if she had to lift her piece of cliff. You wanna drink?

I'm hungry, Clara always says, you wanna eat? Or else I'm hot, you wanna open the window? She never asks about my wants, persistently limiting herself to proposing that I share hers. As if I didn't have my own existence—But did I really have one, in the end?— As if I had become a natural outgrowth of her, a far extremity of the self that one generally took care of, unless one inadvertently forgot.

While she is going to look for the glasses, I lean over the void that is the living room whose dimensions irresistibly call out for twirling dresses music sounds of glasses clinking light conversations on the side under the stairs amorous intrigues in the midst of connecting or undoing themselves with sweetness with nostalgia with ease . . . My head is spinning a bit. I lift it up to contemplate the string of little living rooms where you have to go up one or two steps, to turn, to descend. The gigantic fire that now crackles in the hearth throws its light on the silhouettes stretched out all around on the sofas meant for talking for falling silent for shying away maybe, but always with such fluidity . . . The fluidity of rich people Of people whom one would call 'comfortable', doubtless because of their measured gestures, unversed in need and clumsiness, never tangled up or out of place, always precise. Oh, Clara's grace as she moves about in the kitchen That lightness that belongs to another realm That—yes—that beauty that air of nobility that never overflows, nor overdoes it, that knows its measure its harmony, its right note.

Surreptitiously desperate, I return to the side of the cliff that juts out into the main living room, clean as a polished rock, with its streams as pure as spring-water recycled drained by magic under the floor, its strata of grey of white of grey-blue, of ochre sometimes. Its spangles of mica its crevices and its ridges . . . A real mountain in miniature, entered the room as though it had burst through the wall. And just on the other side of the windows, the same cliff that continues, but this time in its wild state, with grass and shrubs and the wind that passes over it.

I know that if I lift my head my gaze will take in the little balcony that serves the bedrooms, each with its bathroom its coloured tiles its little dish for the soap its chrome its unbearable shininess of things perpetually new and clean, inalterable, made for human beings with skin that's eternally smooth and just matte enough just elastic enough, for whom each day hundreds of litres of water is needed, mountains of lather, and those delicate essences that one only finds in specialized stores and of course exorbitantly priced, that don't stink, that insidiously penetrate you right to your soul and transform you into humanoid mutants by whose contact one becomes almost airborne almost drunk almost detached from the world—from the truth, with its brutal odours sweat fried fat burnt coffee bleach diluting piss.—

Come, says Clara whose voice never shatters the silence but leans into it confidently, with complicity. Come, we'll go cook ourselves some eggs anyway. I'm hungry, aren't you? And your tomato juice, you're not drinking it? I sniff the tomato juice while stopping myself from vomiting. Leave it, says Clara, I'll drink it. What do you want, then, some water? Bubbly or flat?

I burst out laughing because of Ariane who asked me the other day if I had ever drunk bumpy water and what that could even be.

The kitchen is a 'laboratory'. It's rational. It's glacial. It's surgical. But in the end it's a kitchen—with a counter, like in a bistro, but less vulgar—and I circulate there almost at ease. I find a sort of voice—prudently, because if I let it go, my people's voice, my voice of the streets, everything is going to explode in it, that's for sure. To begin with the immense skylights in the living room that look onto the flat part of the cliff, and beyond to the sea.—

Why did you bring me back here?

Because, says Clara turning the omelette over, this is my house. Because I want you to love it, at least, I would like that. And because I hope to see some things, while watching you walking in my house . . .

I stop myself from asking What things? Especially as Clara has fallen into a sort of worrying or guardedness, an uncertain and ill-at-ease state in any case, where the cooking of the eggs comes in for part of it, but perhaps not. And as she turns off the gas under the burner, she murmurs as if to address some absent witness: —No one ever comes here. Almost no one. Almost never . . . In the end I ask myself if this place exists. You want regular bread or whole wheat?

Then, we cleaned. There were dead insects everywhere in the bathtubs—I left them to Clara—, some horribly dried-out mice in the traps, droppings everywhere, and all the sheets were moth-eaten as well as a good part of the coverlets. I thought that we would end up crying and deciding to sleep downstairs rolled up in the carpets. I'm sorry, Clara said, I didn't realize

. . . Leave it, Jean-Jacques was right, it's a dead house . . . Dead.

Then I felt myself inflated with a Herculean strength that straightened my back, enlarged my shoulders to four times the usual dimensions. It was made of anger, of an invincible spirit of contrariness, and of a sort of exaltation too, like in movies when all is lost and the hero cries Onward!

I began by going to feed the fire, that Clara had forgotten. I added logs the way you're supposed to, by crossing them and without spacing them too far apart, as she had taught me to do at the beginning of the evening. Then I promised Clara that we were going to sleep in clean rooms. In the beds. In the sheets, there must still be some that were usable. And I shook brushed scrubbed aired everything that presented itself to me, including spider webs ooh la la, galvanizing Clara who tore up the cloth wherever the mice had chewed. In the end, we had enough to make two beds, a big one and a little one. It was two in the morning, a good warmth reigned everywhere, and the place shone.

I can scarcely believe, said Clara, that anyone could work harder, even in a pioneer camp! What a to-do! What an evening . . . You will forgive me for it one day? She was in my arms I rocked her I tucked her in, she was numb with fatigue. If I had slipped in with her in the big bed, I know that she would not have pushed me out. But I didn't want it to happen like that, in distress and exhaustion. I went to sprawl out on the little bed in the other room, where I immediately slept like an unfeeling, soulless brute.

When I came out of my room, Clara was coming down the stairs, her bust seeming to rise up from an immense black skirt that came down to her ankles, brushing the edges of the stairs.

—Good morning. What's the weather like?

—Don't start asking questions already, said Clara sitting down on a step, the fullness of her skirt gathered between her knees. I warn you, I don't want to answer a single one.

Anyway, all it took was one look through the immense skylights: it was raining. I said that in the end this piece of the cliff was going to slide into the sea, and the house with it.

—It's true, Clara said hugging her wrists between her knees, that will surely happen . . .

And then, as one offers an excuse without any certainty of its validity:

— . . . But everyone will be long dead by then . . .

I sat down at Clara's feet, on the step below. She took my head on her knees. The rain swirled in sudden whirlpools on the skylight. Long dead . . . Clara sighed again while slowly closing the fingers of one hand on the nape of my neck. What are you thinking about?

—Nothing.

—Me neither, said Clara, I can't think of anything. Absolutely nothing. It's extraordinary.

I have my face in the fabric of that skirt that's bunched up between her thighs and that smells of verbena A dry odour An odour of the South that I'm not familiar with I have Clara's fingers that weigh on the nape of my neck with an insistent softness As if they're very slowly pressing just into the skin into the flesh even unto the skeleton And I hear the rain all up high like a world in furore but far away, that could no longer reach us. Then I think of the cliff to the sea that gnaws below. And I want to wait for centuries, for the earth to open up and swallow us soldered thusly grafted having made flesh and skin as one by no longer moving.

I try in vain, I can barely remember what we did with that day, except for a little cooking and some very run-of-the-mill conversation. Maybe after all we didn't do anything else, because it was raining buckets on the cliff. I can see the fire. Clara's hands before the fire, the contour of her fingers having become translucent. Clara's gaze, large and sombre and tense like a cloth that the wind at times filled and let go. What was there behind that darkness where the shifting winds left their mark? Behind that smile that spread then died in imperceptible trembling? I believe that I was always a bit too modest with Clara. I ought to have squared my shoulders and plunged in, like I had plunged into the filth of the bedrooms the night before in the evening. Instead of responding to her like a good little schoolgirl.

—You know what you're going to do, after the bac?

—Yes. Go to college for history. I'm looking also for a job that I could do at the same time . . . I think they might take me as a monitor at the boarding section of the high school.

—But . . . Why not literature, since you . . .

—No. Absolutely, not. I don't want to explain to people what's in books. You understand? No one can decide for others what's in a book.

—I understand, Clara said smiling at me At the last second she let fall her hand that had been reaching towards my knee. History, that's not a bad idea . . . There's geography with it, right?

—Yes. That, that'll be in memory of Ariane. She always wants to go far away . . . To America . . . To Timbuktu . . . She always had her head full of exotic names, Ariane.

—It's funny, said Clara, to hear you talk about Ariane in the past tense . . . As if . . . As if she or you had already left . . .

I got angry. I said that I had absolutely not spoken in the past. Why in the past?

—Excuse me, said Clara. I must have misunderstood. It was because of the 'in memory of' . . . No, it's too late to put on another log. We have to let the fire die out now.

All that sounded like a condemnation. I sought out Clara's hands to feel less alone. She surrendered them to me with such reticence that I immediately let them go. Then it was she who took up mine as though to erase something.

—Clara. I want you to tell me what you SAW, since last night . . . Anyway if . . .

Without looking at me, Clara raised her shoulders with a guilty or weak air, confessing that she still didn't know what feeling she had for me. Then she gave me back her gaze, like a black veil smooth and stretched taut by the wind.

She basically said that she didn't know, that she didn't understand the nature of this thing. That it was maybe . . . maybe well a sort of sad non-love, growing in symmetry with what one must call my sadness, each one aggravating the other and not resolving anything, but was it really necessary to resolve?

I wonder who would have the guts to tear someone's heart to pieces—to break their heart in two, as one says—to hear oneself rejecting someone in such a strange way. The fact is that I didn't have the strength for it, busy as I was trying to unravel the meaning of this 'sad non-love' that had not failed to make Ariane explode:

—It's going well, yes? bellowed Ariane. What's that mean, then, logically? It means that she would really like to like you but that she can't, so she feels bad about it Yeah right she doesn't give a shit about anyone! Tell me, who has the right to say that to anyone? Who? How long are you going to be able to put up with that?

I honestly believe that no one knows what they can put up with or not. I realized this as I listened to Ariane yell. In watching her go quiet and examine me as if I had suddenly changed race or even species.

And now what are you gonna do? my little sister Ariane had said, in a softer tone that was almost frightened, but still fighting however like a valiant little warrior. You can clearly see that she doesn't give a shit, about you You're going to stay planted there all the same staring at her in perpetuity I wonder how anyone can be so stubborn as to love someone who really doesn't give a shit . . .

I said to Ariane that she'd do well to mind her own business I said that surely I would leave.

—Leave? Where to? asked Ariane scooching her butt on the sidewalk to get closer to me in a sudden burst of hope.

—I don't know. Someplace else. Far.

Ah! said Ariane as if she could see me retaking human form, ah, I knew it! I'll go with you, we'll have a wonderful life . . . After all, your Clara, she's nothing but an ordinary dentist's wife. She wasn't worth it, in my opinion. So where you wanna go, huh?? Marseille? Amsterdam? Singapore! Or maybe Maracaibo? They make me dream, those names! We'll go by trains, ships —aeroplanes are too expensive—Anyway, we'll do what you want, but if you don't have ideas . . .

As soon as I could get a word in edgewise I said to Ariane that we weren't going anywhere. In any case, not together. That nobody could carry her little sister around with her, her whole life, and that she had to understand . . .

—Oh! said Ariane in a reverse scooching of her pants along the sidewalk, oh, don't wear yourself out, I get it.

On that note she got up, dusted off her ass, and looked down at me, coldly.

—Carry around! Don't bother, I'll carry myself around, ya big dummy! And maybe I'll be the first to go. But don't think you can come back one day and find me, I warn you.

Maybe I ought to have taken Ariane's warning seriously. Ariane who sang everywhere, in a piercing voice:

'I will go to En-glaaaaaaaaand
To see the biiiiiig shiiiiiiips
That go round the eaaaaaaarth
As the little biiiiiiiirds do . . .'

and who nudged me with her shoulder, as if to make me stand up straight, when I was miserable in the face of Clara's insensitivity:

'I lo-ove you, you lo-ove me, we lo-ove each
other
Until the end of the eaaaaaaarth . . .
Because the Earth is rouuuuund . . .
My loooooove, don't worry,
My loooooove . . .'

I stupidly believed that she was teasing me, that she was too small to understand. And then I was infuriated by that refrain that followed me around in the house in the street in the bus without end without end, like a permanent mocking of my very singular sadness.

—You can't change the record?

—Why? said Ariane. It fits the current mood. You oughta sing too, it vents frustration. I will go to En-glaaaaaaaand, tra la la la . . . la la! . . . You comin', Abel? It's a waltz La la la . . . la-lai-reuuu, La la laaa . . . lalala! You waltz like a bear-cub, my cutie-pie!

—I thought we were going to America, wondered Abel whose boots stopped him from waltzing correctly and who, in any case, didn't like to dance.

—It's the same, explained Ariane to Abel dragging and pushing him   America England or Timbuktu, as long as it's SOMEPLACE ELSE who gives a shit!

Ariane was right. We ought to have left. All of us. While there was still time. While we could still believe in it, not like my mother with Australia which now she hardly ever talked about any more, satisfying herself with a shrug of the shoulder, always the same one—Switch shoulders, counsels Ariane, or else it'll end up getting stuck—every time we tease her on that very subject.

Someplace else, under a different sun, in unsettled places, new, temporary, a better layout for our lives might have been possible. How to know? We might have even been able, who knows, to bring along my mother—my father, no. Surely not. This is an unmoving man, who breaks everything without even trying as soon as he moves.—But my mother, maybe, after a good rest-cure in Australia cleverly orchestrated. At least we might have tried. But we were too little. We were always too little, to start with me, the eldest: I was the first to leave the others, Abel wasn't fooled, by looking forward to SOMEPLACE ELSE for me alone. It was from me that the signal came. From me—whom Abel denounced, in all lucidity, against all evidence.—And it's really me who ought to answer for what's starting to look unambiguously like a crime.

III

'The essential is to go on squirming forever at the end of the line, as long as there are waters and banks and ravening in heaven a sporting God, to plague his creatures, per pro his chosen shits.'

Samuel Beckett (*The Unnamable* 71)

Because then the course of events suddenly sped up. At Margot's house, we only made brief polite appearances: as for me, I had too much work. Ariane was spending all her free time on her interminable grooming, and Abel was killing his free time on the Perfect Crime in comics.

In an outburst of rebellion, I sometimes dared to attack Clara, for the pitiful pleasure of ransacking the little membranes—those floating fibres, impalpable, that connect individuals to each other, that fragile fabric of looks and half-smiles moments of letting go, all things tiny and vulnerable that one ought never expose to the ravages of speech.—

—Why were you interested in me? Were you bored?

—That's it, Clara had said with that smiling harshness that she typically uses to deter intruders. I needed a distraction, what do you want . . .

And a little later, completely out of the blue for those who were unaware of the underground passageways of her conversation:

—Because you think you're funny?

It's Thursday. No dentist. I passed the bac and I'm on vacation. We're going to celebrate that, Clara had said in one of those bursts of enthusiasm that sometimes crack her habitual reserve. Unless it's less a question of reserve than a sort of numbness in which my just being there would plunge her, by a slight foreboding, by a late-blooming sense of caution, I dunno.

Celebrate that, Clara had said. I bet that you've never drunk real champagne. There will never be a better time to be jolly, you're going to have a tremendous life, I can sense it!

My mother—in a fit of inspired madness like she has from time to time—had just given me eighteen white roses for my bac and my birthday combined: a stunt that would have us eating mackerel every day until the end of the month.

I make my mother waltz to the sound of the radio.—I love to dance so much, says my mother, ah la la And of course your father never liked it . . . Let's not even talk about Abel, a dead weight. La la lai-re, la la la . . . Luckily I have daughters . . . And why don't we go dancing once in a while all three of us girls? Oh, I'd let you have your fun. Except you would save the waltzes for me, there's not too many of those . . .

—You mean there aren't any of those at all! guffaws Ariane. You're completely behind the times, Ma.

—The waltz, maintains my mother, holds up against all the latest crazes, don't try to fool me, I was your age long before you were.

I've got your number, my mother said to Ariane who couldn't even argue she was laughing so hard. I've got your number, finally seeming to recognize herself among us, taking root again both a ray of sunshine and looking better. Never fear, doll, I've got your number right here!

Ariane is transforming herself day by day. Long gone, the stories of sailors and trappers, cast off the worn-out, wrinkled, awful pants. Scattered the balls the marbles the fabulous escapades planned out in her head . . . Ariane gets smaller. Ariane reads entire stacks of romance novels, sprawled on a corner of the bed, twisting her hair with a sleepy finger.

—And why don't you suck your thumb, too, while you're at it?

— . . . me the fuck alone, yawns Ariane.

—I found your old pacifier. Apparently they stimulate intellectual effort . . . You want it?

Silence.

—Ariane, listen . . . You're not really gonna sink into a moronic state. Remember what you always said . . .

—Shit, Ariane says to me patiently without interrupting her reading.

She has polish on her nails—Fine, said my mother, I'll allow it, but clear—She frizzes her hair with a wooden fork, plucks the four golden hairs that have sprouted at the edge of her eyebrows, shaves the down on her legs that resprouts right away like Abel's beard, powders her eyelids in blue greases her lips in pale pink, and pierces the linoleum with the point of her heels.

My father complains because of the brand-new linoleum—What the fuck is this shit? YOU ALL walk on nails now?—Always that plural that automatically implicates us all It ain't kids that I've got, it's wolves, vampires And now YOU ALL walk on nails Now we've seen everything! Naturally neither Abel nor I wore stiletto heels, but this is a meaningless detail, WE pierced his lino, never mind which one of us.

My mother defends Ariane, using for her own account a new inclusive plural—We can't do anything about it, it's in style right now. YOU ALL can be so old-fashioned!—That 'you all' that links me for the first time to my father in a common mockery of these frivolities (Abel seeking refuge once again in a state of sour uncertainty) created for us a bond of defiance.

—Was Mom like that?

—I dunno, says my father without raising his eyes from his newspaper Maybe, I didn't notice.

—There, my mother always said, the story of my whole life: he didn't notice. And now we're old farts . . . Oh, my children, enjoy your youth!

A bear, concludes my mother. I've lived with a bear. From certain angles, you look like him, my poor Camille . . .

Lavishly, she covers Ariane with costume jewellery: necklaces bracelets chintzy rings. All that hardware adding to the battalion of vials bottles boxes and pots and various tubes of nauseating perfume, invading the top of the dresser, infiltrating my books—my famous 'damned books' that take up space, gather dust, hinder true order, which are put in place by alignment wiping and elimination.—

The dopey gaze of my little sister Ariane made up like a carnival doll made me want to slam doors.

—Snap out of it! I can see your brain going all soft.

—Mind your own . . . says Ariane from behind her romance novel.

—Leave her alone, bristles my mother. She's at that age.

—That's it, Ariane weighs in stupidly. It's my age.

—It amuses her, says my mother.

—That's it, repeats Ariane in the same tone of a spoiled child. It amuses me. If you think you're all that funny . . .

—It's true, says my mother with a somewhat fearful look, somewhat bothered, towards my table piled up with papers. You're not really happy, for your age, you know . . . You remind me of your father with his newspaper.

—It's true, insists Ariane whose eyes I still can't see. You're both killjoys. Real creeps. You make me want a change of scenery.

Irritated by this eternal comparison to my father, I push aside the piles of romance novels that are blocking my path with my foot. They're nothing but fluff, admit it.

—We know they're full of shit, admits my mother with a slightly guilty look, but what do you expect . . . It gives a different perspective. It's relaxing.

—Yeah, says Ariane wallowing on the bed without a care for her pretty dress, it's really relaxing. Wouaaaah . . .

—If you think, says my mother, that life is fun every day. At least with those you can get some peace . . .

— . . . Not the slightest worry, says Ariane.

— . . . You know that it's going to end well, my mother tells me with a sorrowful look as if I was refusing her absolution out of pure bad faith.

— . . . Life through rose-coloured glasses . . . yawns Ariane. It's cute. It's happy. The Good Guys look like Good Guys, the Bad Guys look like Bad Guys . . .

— . . . You can't get mixed up, says my mother. Nor be demoralized because you didn't understand a word of it.

She smiles at me, as if waiting for a minuscule concession that I persist in refusing her. Abruptly, she laughs, scoffing at me:

—And besides, it's nice, right, Prince Charming marries Cinderella . . .

— . . . And the Boss is in love with the Secretary . . . Mom, I want to be a secretary. I would marry the son who inherits the business, after having proven . . .

—. . . with patience and sweetness . . .

—that the Daughter of the Vice President is a fat cow!

—. . . Greedy and unscrupulous.

—. . . That she's not even a virgin. She had a lover!

—No doubt, says my mother. We'll prove it. I'll help you.

—. . . You'll follow her in secret. You'll gather the Evidence.

—. . . And we'll be rich, doll! Yeah but.

—We'll go to America, says Abel who just came in at the same time as my father. Wait for me before you leave, I'm gonna wash my hands.

—To Australia says my mother, for the benefit of my father back in the hallway. We'll have rings.

—Necklaces. Medals.

—Cars!

—A pet kangaroo.

—We'll be rolling in gold.

—Gold will be rolling off us.

—Like an avalanche, proposes Abel letting himself fall backwards onto the bed. We'll be buried squashed dead under the gold!

—Stop . . . We'll go dancing every night. Waltzes.

—We'll have a pool.

—Horses.

—Guests everywhere. Even in the bathtub.

—Drowned in the bathtub, says Abel. Awful ones. Swollen ones.

—Stop. Naked ones.

—Orchids.

—Dingoes, says Abel in a loud voice.

—You're crazy, they bite!

—Exactly, says Abel. I'll kill them, hiya! With a knife . . .

—A washing machine.

—Some sunshine.

—To dry out the dead dingoes, says Abel.

—Fur coats.

— . . . Made of the skins of dingoes. We can put them everywhere, the dingo skins On the walls On our heads, with their big fur red with blood.

—Silk pyjamas, insists Ariane as if she didn't hear Abel.

—That's a thing?

—Of course.

—And a baby elephant, says my mother in the park. They're cute, baby elephants.

—And servants, adds Ariane. Can't forget that.

I shrug my shoulders:

—Why not slaves?

—All right, says my mother with a great act of generosity, no slaves. From now on, little girl, you'll clean your room yourself.

— . . . When one has principles, says Ariane.

—Dingoes everywhere, Abel insists with a voice that's become crazy As decoration on the walls Dead Throats slit. Hanging by meat hooks, Abel finishes with that cynical laugh that in the end no one can tell if it's sincere or just a perfect imitation, haa haa!

—Cut it out, says my mother. What's come over you?

—Could you shut the hell up, says my father suddenly. It's time for the news. What're we having for dinner?

—Mackerel.

—Mackerel AGAIN!

Obviously. I contemplate the eighteen white roses that are wilting in the big pitcher. Vigorous, brilliant, sumptuous roses . . . Don't sweat it, doll, my mother had said, it's not every day that you turn eighteen and pass the bac. And you have your Future. And I know that you don't like carnations, besides it's true, they seem common . . .

We'll drink to that, Clara had said. Tomorrow is Thursday. Tell your parents that I'm inviting you.

There was a flamboyant sun A sun such as one almost never sees. I was only wearing a thin T-shirt, even thinner since it was worn to the point of being see-through—You aren't going to wear THAT! My mother had protested indignantly. They'll think you have nothing to wear.—But this is the one I like. I left my mother moaning about my lack of pride, because at my age I ought, especially if I was hanging out with decent people . . .

Clara's breasts were in place under my shoulder-blades, burning. Even the wind was hot as it whistled around our bodies en route to the cliff. Easy, easy, said Clara's fingers as they dug into my sides with a sort of complicity or in any case a more intimate contact than usual. And without stopping I would accelerate. In the end she bit me on the shoulder and, from the shock of it, I stopped.

I was afraid, said Clara. Are you crazy, or what? You want to kill us? My T-shirt was torn and underneath I was bleeding. Clara admitted that maybe she had bitten a little hard. But she seemed more surprised than really sorry, when she brought the pieces of the top together to seal them back up. I said that it didn't matter, anyways. That it was super old, that shirt. That my mother had chewed me out. And that I would pay attention, about the speed.

We remounted the scooter, and Clara's cheek came to rest upon the bite mark with extreme tenderness. I was no longer anything but those several square centimeters of skin where Clara's cheek was burning shining searing. I didn't notice anything for the rest of the ride, not even that the sky clouded over.

On arrival, Clara examined the horizon towards the sea, said that we might end up having a real storm, and that she had a present for me.

Don't put on that brutish attitude, said Clara directing her big silent laugh in my face You gave me a fine present, you did, and if my memory serves me well it wasn't even my birthday. It looks good on you.

I gaze in the mirror at a pair of real American jeans that do, actually, look really good on me. You don't hem them, says Clara, you just roll the bottom. Like this. She is bent at my feet, in the middle of her big black skirt that's spread out on the tile floor, busy rolling up the bottom of the jeans, and I let her do it in a state of amazement.

And this, says Clara, this is to replace that T-shirt that I chewed up. It's a real cowboy shirt. Do you like?

—Was that a premeditated bite?

—Stop, says Clara. It went with the jeans. I'm allowed to have premonitions. Change your shirt, now that I'm thinking of it . . . Ooh it's hot, don't you think?

—There, says Clara. Now what's wrong is that your hair doesn't go at all . . . You need it to be very very short, like Jean Seberg, you know? Whew I'm thirsty. You want something to drink?

—Your mother . . . says Clara coming back with glasses full of ice cubes, you think she would have a fit if I cut it for you?

My mother, of course, was more in favour of curls. But my head belongs to me and I offer it to Clara. I let myself be made over from head to toe. I walk barefoot on the tile, like one does with rolled jeans. The locks fall. You can hear the thunder. Here it comes, says Clara, it's going to rain.

It rains. I can't even say that I don't recognize myself, because I've never been anyone in particular: I'm seeing myself for the first time.

You are superb, says Clara with her big black eyes fixed behind me and thrown back at me by the mirror. Do you like how you look, at least?

I smile at Clara and at the stranger in the mirror. Someone else's smile, that goes through me like a flash. In these new clothes that don't even seem new—the height of elegant subtlety—underneath this haircut that no one would dare get and that inexplicably brings out my eyes, I no longer look like someone from my neighbourhood. I changed race and mood. I belong in this setting.

It's raining in torrents. The skylights are rattled by it. The flash of the lightning engulfs us completely as if we were outside, right below it. I lift my head: it's zigzagging everywhere. Then the noise crushes us, as if we were at sea.

—You afraid? Says Clara leaning on my shoulder.

I say no, never. I say it loud, in the middle of claps of thunder echoing indefinitely under the skylights. Never, no. You're stunning, says Clara without making it clear whether she was still talking about the clothes or my exemplary courage.

It's almost night, and we toast. I don't know when the champagne cork flew, nor where. It's the first time that I have champagne in my glass and that my glass is a goblet, thin as a soap bubble. I drink the bubbles that are in the bubble. I watch them rise in Clara's eyes. Who laughs. Clara laughs. Throws me her laugh, practically on my mouth:

—You're right, let's dance, why not! It's a good thing that I thought to bring music. But I didn't know that you knew how to dance. You never said so. Where'd you learn?

—With Ariane.

—Precious Ariane, says Clara, with her string . . . You're funny, your family.

I say no, not especially. Except for Ariane, and maybe my mother, once in a blue moon.

—It's strange, says Clara who's drinking without stopping (like me, moreover) It's strange, I barely recognize you, and at the same time I recognize you even better . . .

We ate light ridiculous things, minuscule corn cobs, giant pickles, little rolls stuffed with sausages, lemon mayonnaise with shrimp and Gruyère in the salad, and we popped a second cork, which seemed natural to me because I was relaxing the more I drank.

—Smile for me, says Clara putting on a record. You so rarely do . . . Come.

She holds out her arms to me. She will always hold her arms out to me. Always. As if to invite me to walk towards her. To walk towards. To walk. And I will always advance in a sleepwalker's daze meeting hands arms bodies whose strange heat—foreign—penetrates me and dilutes me and maybe very lightly denatures me—or reveals a depth in me that I didn't expect of myself. —

It's possible that we danced for hours on end, to blues that would turn your stomach inside out From time to time, we went upstairs to dip our wrists in the rivulets running like mad from the piece of cliff, no longer knowing what they swept along with them.

Don't drink any more, Clara said Or if you do then have some water, you're not used to it. She gathered water from the rivulets in the palm of her hand

and trickled it on the nape of my neck on my eyes on my hair Gently Seriously. Is that better? Camille, look at me, is that better? She had very gently taken off my glasses, as though they were something that separated and that got in the way.

We couldn't hear the thunder any more. We couldn't see the lightning any more. But on the skylight, it was still pouring: such a steady and continuous and torrential rain that you would've sworn would never ever stop.

Don't move, said Clara, I'm going to shut off the record player.

And later—or immediately afterwards—Don't fall asleep on the rug, you'll be better off in your bed, come on. You're okay, right? She squeezes my hair with her palms, to extrude from it the last drops, and my gaze gets lost in the blackness of her eyes like in a complicit night when you feel in harmony with the world. She's so close, radiating heat like an ember, that I wrap my arms around her body That her body yields and envelops me Clara her eyes closed and your mouth finally in my mouth Clara eyes so big that in the end they close as we fall Clara naked and searching for me under the too-tightness of the new pants that in slipping off make a sound like cardboard.

Oh shut up Shut up, I don't . . . No, shut up . . . I drank and I ate Clara's body while crying The water of Clara's body The smell so strong oh my God of Clara I had her teeth against my teeth and on the nape of my neck and on my sides I was sucked devoured dissolved I was rolled grasped smoothed projected in concentric circles in a marvellous succession of chasms I was found again identified licked spread made red hot . . . And I have nothing left from it. Nothing. The body is so forgetful that it makes you want to kill yourself.

I remembered almost nothing from that night, except an enormous internal wave eternally rising, with the desire to unfold again and again and again, sweeping aside all that stands in its path and gets stuck and obstructs and prevents my absolute and vertiginous need for the naked, shining, wide-open body, of Clara.

I don't know any more which surface to cling to in order to rediscover a horizon or even just a little space. No matter which side I turn to, from then on, it's a vertiginous mountain peak. And me I'm below, twisting my ankles between the rocks, knowing that no one will ever come—will never be able to come again—to finally throw me a rope.

But Listeeeeen! yelled my little sister Ariane into the telephone This thing with Abel, seriously are you doing it on purpose or what   Do you realize that I'm completely overwhelmed here, and this is not a good time to come telling me your bullshit stories . . . Camille   CA-MILLE! You listening to me?

—Yeah. I'm telling you . . .

—NOT ONE WORD, my little sister Ariane yelled again   I don't believe one word of your little story   Listen Camille, let's not get upset here   Listen to me carefully: if it's really YOU that killed Abel, if it's really TRULY you, you can rest assured that he's easily resuscitating himself as we speak . . . And if I were you, I wouldn't turn my back on him, you understand what I'm getting at? Do you get me?

—Ariane, I'm begging you. Abel is dead. DEAD. Because I'm telling you that . . .

—Well go in peace, said my sister suddenly calm. Heaven help you   May you be blessed unto the seventh generation, as for me, I've got an appointment with the paediatrician for Camille . . . Just between us, she's very cute.

—Camille?

—No, said Ariane, the paediatrician.

And then after a short silence, in a voice turned cold again that cut like a knife: Anyway YOU aren't the one who's gonna make a fuss about it, are you? Okay, sure, catch you later . . . Listen Camille, I don't know. Yeah, maybe. Maybe I'll call you back, I don't know, I have to think.

And my sister Ariane hung up.

I wasn't destroyed however Only chipped A thin stream of coldness came to me over—inside—through the gap My shell, or what served me as such, has been broken My body feels cold as though in a persistent draft The anguish from outside And at the same time I am helping to break, with my own hands, that which kept me warm What kept me inside, closed in.

To be thrown outside To help with the ejection oneself Not knowing, maybe, that the world will always always be cold Not knowing what one has done What one will do to others Being irresponsible, absent Being in the void.

—Listen, said Clara.

Completely in the void In those weightless spaces where there is no longer any up or down.

— . . . In any case, said Clara, I ought to have told you . . . Camille Oh Camille . . . I know all this doesn't make any sense, but you mustn't see it as . . .

Not seeing. Turning towards that which moves or does not move or not yet Not understanding Not knowing.

I can't believe, said Clara, I truly can't believe that after all these years we could become strangers to one another, that doesn't make any sense. Listen, Camille Be reasonable It's been so long that I've wanted this baby. That's how it is. There's nothing I can do about it. Camille, come on, say something . . .

I know, said Clara. About the other day, I don't know what . . . Really I don't know. Really.

I say brutally that it was the storm. The wine. The music. The torrential rain on the skylights. A fit of sleepwalking. The Devil's sneeze . . . Or the craving of a pregnant woman.

She says, finally turning away her big black eyes which each of my words seems to bounce off as though from a screen after sinking in slightly, that I might deserve a slap. But she doesn't give me one.

She says without looking at me that she will never forget, in any case, that she has a memory . . . It's like a jewellery box, something precious. I would kill her, if I were capable of killing someone. And afterwards she murmured, very very softly, without daring to touch me or to even come closer: Pardon me.

As if she had gently bumped into me in a crowd Or else had mistaken me for someone else, by accident.

I can still see the look in Clara's eyes when I speak to her harshly—or only, afterwards, brought on by weariness, with a certain abruptness.—A dark gaze Immobile As if unfolded, stretched, offered even, on the entire available surface That receives words like blows Where the impact of the word-stones—word-rocks—word-bombs—is visible in imperceptible cracks craters sudden hollows immediately smoothed out by an effort to pull tight somewhere near the edges. Clara's gaze is an immense black veil, shaken by contrary winds, always on the brink of splitting tearing breaking, but that doesn't break. That endures.

Meanwhile Ariane is still growing, growing more and more, in that obstinate conformity that she flaunts like something original, as though in a spirit of contradiction.

—Drop your gloomy attitude, said Ariane combing her eyelashes in the mirror above the dresser, you're not the only one who's in love, it's no big deal. You're not really gonna chase after this Clara your whole life, right . . . Are you serious? She's your One True Love?

And by the way, said Ariane while separating her clumped-together eyelashes with the point of a needle, which always turns my stomach, and by the way, your Clara, isn't she just a little pregnant around the edges, right now?

I tell Ariane to leave me the fuck alone, and anyway she's putting too much on.

—Too much what?

—Mascara. You look like a clown.

And now my father had said with a nauseated glance towards the top of my head, now here THEY are dressing up like convicts or sailors . . . Aren't we done with all this shit, yet?

All the same, said my mother behind my father's back, I'm not agreeing with him, but it's true that it's funny looking that haircut. What's come over you? And besides I told you so, everyone thinks you have nothing to wear . . . What's that make us look like, huh?

—And what about your sister? Ariane says to me.

—She tarts herself up with all the colours on the palette. She looks just great.

—She's got a date, what would you expect. The boys like something eye-catching . . . Mmmm . . . You can't go for subtle, they'll never notice you.

—Who's the date with?

—With a guy, says Ariane spinning around to make her skirt flare out around her hips like she was still ten years old. Isn't my dress cute?

With both hands, she pulls on the width of the skirt so I can appreciate its fullness, and turns more slowly:

—It's a real party dress. Mom, she really is nice.

—And him, is he nice?

—Who?

—The guy.

—They're all nice, says Ariane sticking her heel in the linoleum in order to slow her rotation, of course!

—So what's special about this one?

—He's got a super ride, says Ariane after slyly giving it some thought.

—And it's the ride that you're in love with?

—Stop giving me shit, said Ariane who was now busily polishing her nails. I don't want to be a widow without a corpse, ME. I wanna have fun, see the world, to . . . It ain't so bad, to be loved, anyway . . .

—But YOU? You love him?

—I looove him, you lo-ve me, we will looove each other . . . Until the end of tiiiime!

—I'm talking to you.

—Yeah yeah, said Ariane, I love him, otherwise I wouldn't go out with 'im . . . But he's the one who's fallen hardest, if you want to know the truth, and it's best that way if you want my true opinion . . .

Because, said my little sister Ariane with a sort of absolutely inexplicable anger or resentment or rancour, because, listen up, all this shivering-in-the-North-Wind-which-slowly-freezes-my-tears, that's not my style, not mine.

If someone doesn't love me, yelled Ariane, I drop 'em, I cross 'em out, I tear out the page And I tear it to pieces. As insurance. In case someday I'm lame enough to try to patch it back together. You dig? I decided that I will be HA-PPY. You hear me? And I will be. Even if I have to bust some balls. That's how it is.

Did I shock you? Inquires Ariane after a brief moment of silence, and in a suddenly subdued voice.

I say no. That she doesn't even know what she's talking about. That she has a thread on her pretty skirt.

—Got it, said Ariane twisting herself around to get the thread off, I was always too young, and a little dumb. But its only dummies who are happy, so that's good for me.

She smiled at me rather sadly in the mirror. I wanted to rub off some of that ridiculous make-up To smear with a kiss all that too-black eyeliner gooping up her eyelashes To knock down the edifice of teasing and hairspray that she called a hairdo To drag all of it under the shower, spike heels, nylon stockings, painted nails, party dress, foundation and accessories included. My little sister Ariane finally stripped and clean and singing buck naked under the spray—squalls and squalls of spray!—

'Chiiiil-dren of the earrrrth
Doooon't give a shit abouuut God . . .
La la la la, la lai-reuuuu . . . '

—Bye bye! said Ariane. Now, I'm really late.

So I said, like the idiot that I will be in perpetuity:

—Have a good time.

Me, I wanna live, said Ariane, you get it: LIVE!—and she repeated it to me over and over. Threw it in my face. Slapped me with it to resuscitate me.—

Live, she didn't really know what that means, except that it had to be in motion and full of kick Like before, when we would play marbles when we stole flowers when we ran until we were out of breath under the grey sky making her lasso whistle as if it were bright and sunny out   Or how our voices sail out the window first thing in the morning:

'The loooo-verrrs of Haaaaa-vre
Don't need the seeeea . . . '

The sea, where I went by myself, the last week of September—Ariane was still very busy, Abel hated the water, and except for Clara, I didn't have any friends.—I saw Clara as little as possible, revolted by that belly that was starting to poke out decisively under her clothes and that I considered a personal offence. Naturally, I didn't tell Ariane anything any more: she would have howled again with that new, short-tempered, and vulgar laugh that I dreaded like a toothache.

The summer had been pretty rotten, as usual, but that last week of the holidays was beginning to look like a heat wave. Everyone was squashed against one another at the beach. And I wandered in the desert of the crowds with the intermittent desire to throw myself in front of a car.

Gerda was so blond—her eyes barely less blond than her hair, while her eyebrows and her body hair were literally transparent—that I looked at her like a ghost.

She smiled at me, then asked for a light. I didn't have one. She was reading a book in French, spoke with an accent that reminded me a little of Gertrude's, but a bit more distinguished in any case. She was on vacation, and was leaving the next day for her country where the sea is very cold, yes, much colder than here, really very very. We talked about books. Because of the sun and her accent lightly highlighting the words, you could've believed yourself somewhere else, in a country where fantasy was possible, where chance was mischievous and teasing. No, it's true, I didn't have a light . . . She could have asked someone else, but we didn't think of that. Then her hand placed itself on mine on top of the mat A soft and imperious hand that was at the same time fearful, supplicating The hand of someone like me. Fallen from which planet? A slow and burning liquid trickled suddenly from deep inside me. I sat up on my knees to stop it from flowing too quickly, from disappearing into the sand.

I brought Gerda to the forest, the only place I could think of, the only one possible. It was long and complicated, we had to change buses Walking in town with our crotches heavy with blood pulsing like when you're thirteen/fourteen years old and you would put a stake in there to calm it to kill it to cure it, who knows . . .

Afterwards, it was as if her skin couldn't stop the sun As if it went straight through her She, the white one, the naked one The absolute opposite of my beloved with dark hair with eyes like the fluid night with her lips delicately painted . . . I am thinking of absolutely nothing. Not even of the bugs crawling under the leaves Or rather, if I do think of them, it's as if I were in another world, one that is softened and hazy, friendly and approximate, where I go when I take off my glasses, and where I feel myself so far out of reach that I am barely inside myself.

I remember the sun. The sunlight above all, it's strange. The sunlight on my head and my back and the movement of her features And also I remember a welcome that seemed perpetual—a good, wide-open friend—when I snap out of it afterwards, dazed by the brightness there she is, crouching and getting dressed again already, she again lets my hands approach and sink in deep lose themselves and swim indefinitely in the endless smooth water of her body.

We didn't pronounce any but light approximate words Come I love you Yes Again. After, she clung to the trunks of trees, as if attracted to them by magnetism, in a kind of intimate recognition, of fervent complicity. I watch her. Luminous. Drinking in the sun through her pores and shining it out through her eyes through her teeth through her hair . . . Her skin, free of any scent of eau de toilette or deodorant had the scent of a sea creature drying in the sun. Her belly was muscled like that of a small boxer.

I don't know if I could have loved her. Maybe I should have tried, instead of passing as though sleep-walking through her transparency that calmed and that dispersed. Because today I ache for her endlessly, like the strong perfumed water of some mountain stream.

Afterwards she led me to the campground where she had pitched her tent in the company of some friends. A dozen women of all ages, in shorts or in jeans, blondes or brunettes but all with eyes almost too luminous, their teeth in the sun like their skin A sort of communal smile, irrepressible.

They sat me in the middle of them They spoke to me very gently in their incomprehensible language They offered me beer Coke fruit juice all the while continuing what they were doing some peeling vegetables others washing them some cutting their toenails a little off to the side others distributing straws for drinking. One of them stubbornly scrubbed some jeans in a basin of soapy water ridiculously too small for this operation, all the while watching the clouds. They offered me cigarettes that I smoked while I too contemplated the clouds through the branches of the apple trees Soft voices That wouldn't disrupt the peace of the evening That on the contrary participated in it Infinite tranquillity, security of gestures: no man, apparently, was expected. There was no urgency anywhere.

I watch them talk to each other brush against one another smile at each other—always this incredible smile, that seemed to come up from the depths, scattering itself on the friend and the friend of the friend and regenerating itself as it went along Exploding fading out as if submerged in a subterranean passage reappearing farther along in other eyes on other lips An infinite circulation of sweetness of tenderness of complicity . . . —I watch them touch each other make a pathway displace the one who's in the way push away a hair that is bothersome or an elbow or a knee or a rump, with the same delicacy as if they were untangling the stems of a fragile plant muddled by the wind.

I feel dark and heavy. A real paving stone from a cemetery.

A woman of about forty—one of the most high-spirited, the ones laughing the most—began to dip her straw in the water from the laundry and to make bubbles. She saw my look. She laughed, caressed my hair while making quite a speech to me in a tender and ironic voice.

She says, translates Gerda, that you are a big, serious girl . . . Why so sad? She says that when she was young she had so many brothers and sister who were even younger that she never had the time to do this. She says that you can't understand . . . that she did everything backwards. She says that you are surely intelligent. She says that one day you will do the same as her. She says . . . No, nothing.

And since I insist on knowing: She says that you ought to unbutton the collar of that shirt a little, you look like a little lawyer!

Uncertain as to the colour of my cheeks, I unhooked the collar of my shirt. And that woman, who was my mother's age and who looks like a wind-blown adolescent, leans forward and brushes my lips with her burning and sisterly mouth.

—In our country, Gerda explains precipitously, we kiss everyone like that when we like them a lot, even children . . .

To show that I've understood clearly, I caress the hand that had stayed resting on the nape of my neck. I want to stay with them. To leave with them To sleep in their warmth in the sound of their voices. Then I say that I have to go back, that otherwise my mother will alert the police the hospitals the firemen and even the morgue . . . Gerda translates translates translates They say that all mothers are like this. Her, she has kids and her too And her They say that you should go They say that you can write to them if you want That you can even come visit us if you want They say . . . *Bye, Cameye, bye . . .*

They enveloped me in their arms in their hair They covered me in their luminous, laughing gazes They put their lips on mine with fervour with tenderness with lightness with good humour And with gravity, too, some of them.

I left, with in my pockets several addresses each more improbable than the last and a little flame in the centre of my body. Then it was windy at the bus stop: I buttoned the collar of my shirt again and I curled up like the wick of candle that snuffs itself out in its own wax.

Autumn. The squish of soggy leaves underfoot. The sound of rain against the windowpanes. A gloom whose weight moves in as if forever, limiting the horizon to that eternal coming and going of clodhoppers beneath the downpour, in the puddles, with the tail of the raincoat turned up by a wind riddled with raindrops.

The winter is like autumn, by the way, or almost. And the spring like winter, except for the promise of nice weather the fog here smells of gas because of the refineries.

At night, I watch over the sleep of high school girls who are the age of my little sister Ariane but whose development is stuck in childhood: they still cry over a couple of hours of detention. During the day, I go to the university, or else I work in my room where I wage an endless fight for space with Ariane's vials and jars, with her romance novels that are starting to gather dust where they lie but that she keeps as relics, not allowing, in her fits of sudden vindictiveness, one to move them even the smallest millimetre.

On my little old school desk, I barely have enough elbow room, and my mother laments not being able to 'tidy up' as one ought.

As for your bedroom, my mother had said, I was kidding, the other day. I don't mind doing it, you know, I'm used to it . . . You do your work. Try to get to the bottom of that pile of papers before night time, I noticed that you don't sleep much, that ain't good.

And anyway, said my mother pushing Ariane's vials to one corner of the dresser so as to be able to dust the rest, it wouldn't get done to my standards, I know you. I really like a room that's just been done to look like a room that's just been done, and not a pigsty . . .

So get to work, said my mother pushing me towards my chair, it won't help me a bit to have you standing around in the middle There You, you're an intellectual And I dunno how that happened, because we never had one in the family before, but what d'you expect . . .

— . . . It's like everything else, said my mother shaking her dust rag out of the window It's like cops priests and soldiers: it's not really our thing, but you need 'em . . . And then if you could earn your living like a man, that wouldn't be a bad thing: it would be good to not depend on anyone, to be able to cut out when you've had it up to here . . . Me, I'm all for it.

—Do you think your sister will get her Certificate? says my mother while closing the window.

—Long as she wants it . . . If she gives a shit . . .

—Don't talk like that, said my mother. School, it's not for everyone . . .

—It's not that, Ma. Something's happened to Ariane.

—What?

—I dunno. Suddenly she's gone crazy.

—Stop! said my mother brutally opening the window again as if we were going to suffocate. Your sister is perfectly normal. She's like everybody else. You're the one who . . . Who thinks everyone's a total imbecile!

I say nothing more. I gaze at my handouts without seeing them. I'm hurting as though from afar, as though my corpse were being harmed.

—My poor little one, says my mother encircling me suddenly in her arms from behind the back of the chair I don't know where you're from, but you're not from here . . . I mean . . . It's not here that you ought to come from. You always seem like you're tied down, here.

I pull my mother onto my lap. I tell her that it's not true, that I really am from here. Absolutely. That I am one of hers, who would have left for Australia, just as . . .

—Oh! says my mother with a wan smile, Australia . . .

—Kangaroos, Ma!

—Elephants! Says my mother with a glimmer of light coming back deep down in her eyes.

—But there are no elephants in Australia, Mom.

—Not even little ones?

—No. No, not even. No elephants at all, I assure you.

—Well, so you see, said my mother. We did just as well to stay . . . Those elephants, I would've missed them a lot.

I plunge into thicker and thicker books More and more dull I swallow up even more of them than the syllabus demands. The history of humanity that spends its time betraying each other gutting each other devouring each other, dragging each other's guts through ploughed fields slicing to bloody bits the ones who were their brothers the day before burning the old and the young mounting an attack, in the blood and the shit, on cities already in flames or in ashes . . . To know. To know everything. Above all never to be ignorant of anything ever again.

—But what for? Complains my mother. Those were terrible things, we need to forget them, otherwise you can't live . . .

—Stop, says my mother, you're killing me. We can't do anything about stuff like that, us . . . And I want to know why they teach it to kids like you!

They're deaf. Deaf as you have to be if you want to go on living If you want to do your little house-cleaning with the radio blaring in the background some tune or some ad for toothpaste. Okay on the toothpaste: we don't brush our teeth enough in this area, the kids' mouths are falling apart . . .

My mother goes to turn off the radio and comes back to talk to me We can't do anything about it said my mother It's destiny Men are crazy. Crazy. Every twenty years there's a war It's lucky in a way that Abel is how he is, at least they won't come and take him from me to turn him into a criminal or a corpse under a flag . . . But I'm keeping you from your work . . .

I work. Massacres soon will have no secrets from me, not their causes, nor their consequences which are yet more massacres. And when I lift up my eyes again, I see the eyelashes of my little sister Ariane, stiff like the bristles of a metallic brush, wearing war paint for such a laughable mating dance that I feel my veins contract and my blood forced through them. Is that all that they teach girls—girls where we're from, NORMAL girls—in that vo-tech that produces future stenographers: the art of painting oneself like a cartoon and twisting one's ankles with skill and good humour? Or has Ariane become an idiot?

Ariane, listen for a sec . . . Ariane . . . And Ariane says that I'm really bugging her and it's really shitty of me, especially right before she's going out dancing. Only a couple of months ago, me too I used to dance in a state of unconsciousness and wonder I would still dance if I could So I know I know.

Yeah, yeah, admits Ariane If you knew how little I give a shit . . . Those people there are dead, says Ariane, and us we're alive. ALIVE! And no matter what you can tell me about people who've been dead for twenty years or three thousand years, it won't bring anyone back anyway . . .

I know. And it won't stop the next ones from jumping on each other full of hate and exaltation as if it were the first time. Even us we used to play at war We thought it was so funny to be prisoners and to say nothing when tortured But we often escaped, and everyone refused to die because that wasn't any fun. Maybe men never grow up. Maybe they all imagine that the real bullets are only for the other guys, and that they themselves will come back, with tanks full of flowers and the music, scooping up the girls that press forward shouting bravo and whom they truly deserved, after all . . . History is a useless science, shit. I'm dropping it.

—You're not going to do that, says Clara, seriously!

—What are you going to do? Says Clara whose belly now stretches her dress to the breaking point, and who moves about with her hands under it to protect it from bumps.

I'm out of ideas. I'm going to find others like me, they must still exist, even if I've lost their addresses. And then? I dunno. I'll live with those women We'll talk to each other with smiles in our voices We'll play our own games We'll make soap bubbles smoke bouquets of flowers. And then soldiers will come, who will kill us under any pretext, there always are some—pretexts and soldiers—and it will be consigned to a history book, barely a brief mention, not worth going on about such a minor anecdote, those women didn't even have canons.

You silly goose, Clara says to me moving her whole body awkwardly forward as though to keep me from falling—but she's the one who finds herself off balance, and I catch her with an exasperated gesture—I think you're a bit depressed, Camille Take care of yourself, Camille . . . You hear me.

I slam doors everywhere At my mother's house In the dorm At Clara's house. Except for the girls who hug the walls as soon as I appear—Those Arianes who are retarded but surely successful who make me want to exterminate them—each one treats me as though I'm half powder keg half severely wounded.

It gets so bad that once again I seek refuge at Margot's house where they're gossiping about Marie-who-has-two-sexes who has just finally retired and who is replaced by a youngster with a wooden leg. The youngster is about forty and has a small veteran's ribbon in his buttonhole, if that's all they've found out about him . . . I listen to them and agree with them, conscious of carrying with me insidious, embarrassing baggage: there were all those books that no one was reading at our house. Then there was Clara, that friend who isn't 'of our world'. And finally, my studies that are never-ending, that plunge the Mothers in a sea of confusion—Are you gonna spend your whole life in school?—but they let me off the hook for it all the same, since I pay my bills on my own and since I have the distinction of no longer living off my parents.

They make room for me   Someone offers me super-burnt java   Margot's goatee has gotten whiter   Gertrude offers me her cigarettes or accepts mine with a dark look, lost, unreadable, and as if discreetly intimidated. Micheline yawns over her knitting, and the conversation sinks into its usual rut.

I swallow my coffee. I get the hell out of there. I shove off. Even the purely polite jokes have become unbearable and useless to me: they are dully disturbing. As if each one of the women knew very well that I will never become a Mother like them, at most a lady who will have grown up on the sly at their sides, with no one suspecting a thing, and by mistake one might say And who will force herself to pretend to be talking to them to make like she was 'down-to-earth'.

My visits, all the same, make them happy, as if it were honourable conduct that they should be grateful to me for. Because people where I'm from are the salt of the earth, and tolerate even betrayal as long as they don't detect too much contempt in it. At Margot's, there is always a cup waiting for me, I know it. But it's just a little bit like the cup of a ghost.

Elsewhere it's the same thing, just the opposite. I'm a spectre from the swamps One who has really strange 'motives' as they say, and who walks either too near or too far from the ground but in any case never at regulation height: the Great Men don't interest me, I made the mistake of saying so. I stupidly worry about the unwritten history of anonymous people That still-developing mass of humanity Generous sometimes Often infantile Heroic Limited. Those people who rise and overflow and in part at least are scorched like milk over the fire: without knowing it and without understanding any of it.

Nonetheless they make wars and revolutions at least as much as the Great Men. And I who have grown up in the homes of these foot soldiers of History, I have to do right by them, I'm not sure how. I know they didn't ask this of me and that they won't return the favour, all of them Robert (my father) Odette Aimée Margot or Gertrude the German who fulfilled their destiny without ever looking for meaning in it, some while bellowing, others while staying silent, without ever figuring anything out. And who, once the murderous shows were over, stunned to still be alive, returned from the wars to their construction sites to their factories and to their kids It's the same old same old.

—And what conclusion do you draw from THAT? A fellow student with a cold and well-educated voice asked me. Everyone knows that!

Maybe. But not enough, I find. I'll have something to say everywhere I go—if I get my diplomas and the right to speak which everyone ought to have—that greatness has nothing to do with fame. That greatness can't be seen with the naked eye. As for the second, it's more the result of a lucky combination of circumstances than of personal skills.

—You ought to have become a philosopher, one of the teaching assistants tossed out to me as if he were throwing me overboard.

—I get you, said Clara with a closeness that we hadn't experienced for a long time. You understand that you can't drop out . . .

But except for those moments when a strange protectiveness emanated from Clara as if I'd been an actual part of her—like she protected her giant belly from jolts or possible accidents—, I felt my life drifting and whirling like a crazy woman, ready to turn inside out to collapse at the first obstacle. And without being able to determine at what point the course set at the beginning had turned out to be false, had been lost: was it from the books—the first ones, or Clara's?—Was it from Clara herself? Or else from that explosion, at Margot's, that had practically dispersed the Mothers, uprooting them from their chairs, scattering them to the four corners of the earth so that they would never again crack up together over a cup of super-burnt java that scorches their fingertips?

Clara can't answer me—she never knew how to answer questions, real ones.—But I know that it's not for her to answer that one. If only she would answer the others, those that I still ask her sometimes when a shooting pain goes through me like an electric shock. But her dark look flees toward the horizon, without her even trying to hide it from me, because Clara is honesty itself and probably I'll finally accept, tolerate, this congenital ignorance regarding her own depths to which she clings as if to a life-saver:

—But why, WHY did you . . . because it was my birthday? Just answer!

—No . . . I don't know.

And afterwards, when I tell her about Gerda-the-blonde, without really knowing why I'm telling her about it, I find myself clued in regarding my own motivations, but never about the hazy, carefully locked-up feelings belonging to Clara. Clara who says, as though she's examining herself and coming to a surprising diagnosis So you see . . . I am not jealous.

—And by what miracle would you be? What would be so strange about not being jealous of someone whom you don't give a damn about!

You're being unfair, said Clara whose gaze had strayed very far on that particular day. When I tell you about my affection, about . . . about my feelings for you, it's as if you were deaf. You don't want to hear about them, because it's not what you demand.

I slammed the door again. One day One day I won't love her any more. I swear it!

And now, years later, I let it float away this dead love whose cadaver, too recently drowned, makes bubbles settling into place. It comes and kills you beneath your ribs like bubbles of emphysema. Very sharp pain, very little, and that disappears with a pop.

And what'd be the use in picking up the thread—necessarily undiscoverable, intertwined as it is with a multitude of others—that leads to what I became, since it's irreversible from now on?

I'd never followed the story of the Mothers very closely.—You were always off to one side, said my mother.—Saint Camille of the Disappearing Act, Ariane would say ever since she started seeing that guy, Richard, the one with the souped-up rig, fasten your seatbelts, we're landing in five minutes!—I didn't like Richard's type of humour coming out of Ariane's mouth. And I never paid much attention to my mother. But I couldn't ignore everything, given how much hell broke loose at Margot's.

—They're going at it, Ariane had said shaking her two hands one after the other, whoo wee, can they ever shout! Can you believe that Mylene ran off with a fella from her factory. Gertrude is fuming mad, she says she's gonna kill him A do-nothing a Whatcha-callit Something nasty, well, he has all those qualities according to her . . . She's fine with her daughter being pregnant, just certainly not with somebody like that. She doesn't want her to keep it . . .

—Stop, you're killing me . . . Who?

—The baby. The fella either, besides. To make a long story short, she threw 'em out.

—The fella?

—No, actually yes. But Mylene along with. And now she's underneath the guy's window, yelling 'Come back right now!'

—To the guy?

—Stop fucking with me, will you. To Mylene. 'Come back, I'm your mother!' What a circus!

—Huh! Mylene's of age, what's the problem?

—Yeah right, luckily for her. The problem? Is with Margot. Can you believe the Mothers, they've been preaching at Gertrude, you've known since forever that this would happen And remember when she was a kid and you'd punish her and she was at the window. Whole days at the window! . . . And now here's Gertrude blubbering, and here's Mom telling her just like that that it's a little late for crying, that you reap what you sow and all that jazz . . .

Here we go again. Ariane's in full 'parrot mode'. But it isn't funny to me any more and I have a headache.

—Oh, listen, Ariane. Stop a sec, you're making my head spin.

—Well fine, my friend, said Ariane turning with an air of waiting to pounce on me. Sure, whatever you say, but you're mixed up in this. 'Cause it's on account of you that they practically jumped all over her.

—Huh?

—Absolutely. Because, we're talking about reaping what you sow, exactly, so get a load of Gertrude who bounces back like a spring, and who tells Mom not to crow, given what she's hatched! Whoooo wee, aye yi yi! If we hadn't gotten between them, Margot Micheline and me, she would have stomped on Gertrude's belly like a kangaroo!

If I were you, said Ariane, I wouldn't laugh so much. I don't know what you did to her, to Gertrude, or what you didn't mean to do to her, it's none of my beeswax, but she's got a damn good grudge against you. Watch out.

I swear, said Ariane, I wonder how you manage it: we barely ever see you, we never hear you, and you fuck things up everywhere you go. To make a long story short. Mom demanded an explanation. She thought at first that she was taking aim at Abel, and she saw red. Then she thought that it was really me, she saw scarlet. But when she understood that it was you, she drew herself up to her full height almost to the ceiling and she exclaimed MY daughter! What do you have to say about MY daughter, who's following her own Path, who's studying like no one else—word-for-word!—who no one has seen hanging around with boys . . . Exactly, yelled Gertrude, let's talk about that. Oh! Boys . . . There's more than just boys on this earth Some people have more twisted ideas, and even show up to make fun of Mothers in their own homes, and first of all you gotta take a good look at her relationships, YOUR daughter's. Look into it, me I'm no cop, and so on and so forth . . .

—Shit! And what's mom say?

—Pheeeww . . . , says Ariane, don' worry. She sees blood red, but doesn't give 'em an inch. She says, go on, laugh it up, she says that at least there's no chance of you getting knocked up by surprise and to look at your Life and your Studies . . . Aaaaand they're out! She was cool, Mom. Amazing. I can't get over it. But that messed with her head, that's for sure. Gonna have to buffer the shock . . .

Well, that's it, said Ariane. Gertrude and Mom aren't speaking any more. The others are all in a tizzy: now's not the time to drop Gertrude, now's not the time to drop Mom, and those two refuse to hear a word about getting together at Margot's. There's crying and nose-blowing on all sides. Gertrude went to Micheline's. Temporarily. And there's no coffee anywhere, I just found out. What a day!

—Look, Ariane said to me seized without warning by a sudden reversion to childhood, look, I'm a flower. And there—look!—a butterfly.

I watch my little sister Ariane who is a flower, turning at full speed on the heel of her pump, her skirt filling up lifting up opening up like a corolla, and then legs joined, the edges of this immense skirt raised straight up above her head between two fingers, its full sweep unfolded, immobile, open, the butterfly.

—Be careful you don't get caught! said my mother shrugging her usual shoulder even though her eyes were red.

There's no sun, and yet it hurts behind my eyes when I look beyond the windowpanes, there where the wind rolls the leaves in the gutters. Images. That's it: too many images, always, in my skull or on the edges or slightly in the background I don't know doesn't matter   In any case there where I only want white Or grey   Well something atonal, restful for the spirit, perfectly neutral for the heart or whatever stands in for one.

A sort of eraser to wipe out feeling and its bloody ropes and its twists and turns and its howls . . .

The guy with the souped-up ride named Richard, we ran into him, Abel and me, at the end of the street. He was feeling up Ariane leaning up against the car door. Abel suddenly went right up to him, his boots swimming around his calves.

—That's my sister, said Abel with an air of ownership.

—That's my girl, said the guy cracking up.

Facing this man—a real man: he was at least twice Ariane's age—Abel immediately lost his composure. When I saw the corners of his mouth were starting to tremble, I looked at the fella from head to toe—unattractive—and I said to Abel Come on let's go.

—I'm coming! cried out Ariane, while I was dragging Abel by his rifle like a big donkey.

We heard the other guy laugh, and I held on more strongly to the rifle that Abel was trying half-heartedly to fight me for.

—She . . . She's gonna get married with 'im? Asked Abel who was already leaking fluids. Huh? She's gonna leave?

I muttered that all that was just a little girl's bullshit, the Big Man, the ride, and all the rest, and that there was nothing to worry about. You might say that I could see the future.

—You sure? Said Abel. I don't like'im, that guy.

I sat Abel down in the kitchen, while waiting for Ariane to come back. His hands started to wring themselves all on their own. He could have used a sedative, but he didn't want to take them any more. And my father wasn't even there—on top of that neither was my mother, no doubt busy debating with her friends about her gripes and her superiority that were keeping her from patching things up with Gertrude.—I should've warned Ariane, so that she didn't come back right away. But we could already hear her whistling in the stairway. And I couldn't sound the alarm.

—Slut! said Abel to Ariane. Slut! What . . . What . . . What'd we do to you?

—That ain't right, no way! said Ariane slinging her bag onto a chair.

—And what about me? yelled Ariane, you wanna tell me what I did to you two?

Abel's fingers were wringing themselves as if their joints had popped out. They clamped onto each other, cracking, slipping, jumping up and clamping on again, literally independent from one another, like so many little serpents with broken coils.

Ariane shut up, her gaze became fiercely frozen, and Abel saw the look that Ariane shot towards his hands. He made an effort to hide them, then he straightened himself up, already stiff and seeping fluid, the brightness of his eyes shining out of his head. He tried to say something again, or maybe it was just a nervous tic of his mouth, but it was too late He was irradiated He was on fire He toppled like a tree, wrecking the chair that we didn't have time to pull away.

—Shit, said Ariane. That must have hurt.

While we dragged him the best we could on a throw rug—he'd become way too heavy for us to be able to lift him up any more—, Ariane said, wiping her forehead with her sleeve with no thought for her make-up:

—D'you see that? I thought he was going to jump me. I was shaking in my shoes. Wha'd I do to him?

I said   Nothing! Give us a fucking break. You really think now's the time to talk about it? We had turned over Abel who was bleeding from his back and his thigh. I ran my fingers through his hair—greasy with dirt, as usual, in search of a possible wound, but there was nothing there. Barely a bump starting to swell.

On that note, my mother arrived, right on time, and she helped us. I wonder Ariane said if people aren't right about him   If he isn't gonna become dangerous   Mom I swear to you, if you'd seen him . . . I thought he was gonna kill me.

—What happened? asked my mother with an unusual sort of severity directed right at Ariane.

—Nothing, shouted Ariane. Absolutely nothing, ask Camille, luckily she was with us otherwise there would've been MORE to tell . . . I REPEAT he's going nuts!

—Don't talk stupid, said my mother to Ariane. Abel is a poor little thing. You, the normal one, you should try to understand. Because if you gang up on him too . . . My poor children, what will become of us!

—If by noticing that he's becoming more and more nuts, that's 'ganging up on him', hammered Ariane, then yes, I'm ganging up on him. Shit, I've had enough! Do me a favour and open your eyes, it's staring you right in the face!

My mother who had never hit anyone slapped Ariane.

—You'll regret that, said Ariane. I warn you, I've had ENOUGH of living in the loony bin.

—If you want another, said my mother calmly, your father'll let you have it.

Ariane shut up, waiting for me to speak. As for me, cowardly, I didn't say anything.

Reflecting on it all from afar, I think I was really shocked by the series of events. Half the week, I worked on my classes until very late at night. The other half, I was sleeping with one eye open. I was watching out for Abel, I was trying to understand Ariane—Oh! without the least epiphany of insight, it's true—I was stewing in a rather repugnant state of suffering (Ariane, as for that, had it right) because of Clara, and the glimmers of insight that I had regarding myself were exceptionally shaky, which is always trying.

But it's a fact: I said nothing.

Spring was a few weeks away. The only way to know it was by looking at the calendar. Abel was back to himself again. He said it was my fault. Hers. Her. Camille. That it was my fault if Ariane . . . And that one of these days he would kill me. His hands were wringing themselves again. My mother, putting her foot down, made him swallow some sedatives. Then she looked at us one by one, Ariane and me and Abel who was still trembling. She said What's this bullshit still goin' on!!

. . . Because I've had enough of it, yelled Ariane. I've had enough of you, shit! Every season we hear talk of bumping someone off Before it was dad Now it's Camille I won't wait for my turn, because I'm warning you: I'll take you out before you can say boo And I guarantee you that I won't miss. Put on your show without me Your crazy bullshit I've had it up to here with it And what's more I'm pregnant I'm getting the fuck out of here, me and Richard. Ciao!

Before we came out of our stupor, she had stuffed two suitcases full—one big and one small—and she had left, a suitcase in each hand, and slamming the door with her foot.

She was going to be fifteen in a few days, we'd already bought her birthday present for her: a valet stand made of polished wood, her dream, especially since it was on wheels.

It's been two years that it's been in my mother's room, because we didn't see Ariane again. Two years that my mother sniffles every day, I hear her, while draping her old clothes on the polished wood. She says that Ariane will come back She's sure, sure: one doesn't abandon one's family like that, especially when one wasn't an abused child. In the meantime, we just received a beautifully printed card, for the birth of the child. It's a girl. Her name is Camille.

—Preg . . . Pregnant! My mother had cried out falling back in her chair. At fifteen, God in Heaven! And now's the time she chooses to leave home! All that for a slap, the first of her life . . . But WHO is going to raise it for her, her little one? Huh? Who?

I told my mother that Ariane would come back within the next half hour, that she had nothing to worry about. . . . I had arrogant and limitless clairvoyance. Abel picked up a book without saying anything, and began to devour some crime. Then my father came home, and we had to tell him.

I wonder where she came from, over and over again, that one, said my father. We've had nothing but messed-up kids, how is that possible.

And with that my mother began to throw direct and indirect hints in his face about the supposed 'heredity' of alcoholics, and luckily my father was sober, otherwise all that would have ended very badly.

Abel raised his nose from his book full of blood and carnage, and asked:

—She's really gone-gone?

My father said That's enough, shit! And a minuscule sparkle began to gleam in the depths of Abel's eyes still so beautiful Too beautiful to be real. How are we supposed to know, said my mother sobbing because it had been hours and Ariane still wasn't back. My poor little one, shouldn't ask questions like that . . . .

—I didn't do nothing, said Abel his gaze wandering, irradiated, suddenly landed on me and pierced me like an electric shock. I didn't do nothing . . .

I watch my brother gather himself up, all his muscles swelling in place as if he were going to begin shouting It's Camille Camille Camille This kid is crazy, said my mother talking to God knows who, stark raving mad! Aren't you ashamed to say such things! While Abel gets up slowly, immense and takes ages to unfold himself under the pressure of the scream that will not come out that is going to strike him coming to its climax, his two hands wringing one another, his eyes white, glazed.

It's my father who took Abel by the shoulders, all stiff, and who laid him down. When he isn't there, it gets difficult for us: Abel is now heavy as a church pillar.

—I really thought he was going to kill her, said my mother. I wonder if Ariane wasn't right, if he's not gonna become . . . He's more and more bizarre, this kid, don't you think?

—Zip it! tossed out my father all the while rubbing Abel's cheeks to bring him back. If you don't shut the fuck up, I'm throwing you all out the window.

They didn't want to bring charges for the corruption of a minor: in addition to everyone's certainty that Ariane was 'corrupt' all on her own, there was also an aversion to the police firmly anchored in the family, each of us was aware that the use of force was the surest means of triggering a chain of catastrophes from which at least one death would result.

Then the infamous Richard wrote an overblown letter in which he affirmed his intention to 'do his duty'. My mother and father gave their consent to the marriage. That way, Ariane might come back, especially since she had gone more than a thousand kilometres, with that damned drifter she had gone and found for herself . . .

Ariane doesn't come back, because of God knows what 'snapped in her head' as my mother maintains, but it's only a matter of days: seems that babies put a woman's head straight. Just have to wait for the treatment to do its work.

On the birth-announcement, there was a telephone number. So my mother said that we would have a telephone too. And in response to our confusion in the face of this excessive luxury that far exceeded our means, my mother explained that first of all she had borrowed the money needed for the installation That second of all we wouldn't use it—well as little as possible—That it was mainly for just in case Ariane . . . And that third of all we were bugging the shit out of her all of us, so there.

My father opened his mouth and shut it without saying a thing He cracked his knuckles and shrugged his shoulders. Abel said How's it work? And ever since the shining, black telephone has been absolutely silent.

In the beginning, my mother would sit in front of it each night, as if in a state of distraction. We could feel her behind our backs, dropping stitches in her knitting, she who, in her lifetime, had never knitted. In the end, my father exploded Threatened to smash the apparatus to a pulp if she continued to sit stuck to that spot looking like she doesn't care while her hands said the opposite He'd had enough enough enough of it All my mother had to do was call first, and for starters Ariane might not've even received the letter . . .

—Impossible, said my mother, it was sent by registered mail. Besides it was a package, there was a romper and booties for the little one.

—Then they'll just have to send the shit back, shouted my father. It's dough spent for nothing. Consider her dead, cry for her once and for all, and leave us in fucking peace! He beat his murderous fist on the table, splitting it cleanly in two.

While listening to my father shouting, I realized that we all knew it: Ariane had committed suicide in silence, without leaving a body and without bloodshed.

And as one recalls the voices of the dead, I still hear my little sister Ariane singing her head off:

'I will go to Eeeeen-glaaaand,
To see the biiiiig ships . . .
La la la laaa la laire,
As dooo . . . the lil birds . . .'

Little shits, my father would say back when I still used to kill him You're all little shits! I ain't got kids, I got snakes vultures . . . wolves!

IV

'They'll surely bring me to the surface one day or another and all then sink their differences and agree it was not worthwhile going to so much trouble for such a paltry kill, for such paltry killers.'

S. Beckett (*The Unnamable* 71)

I always tell stories, my mother was absolutely right to be suspicious. The proof is that it's not even October, it's March, and there couldn't be even one single dead leaf in the gutters. It's the sound of reeds that I have in my ears. Reeds, and not leaves—that anyways I couldn't even hear through the windowpanes—Those leaves that called forth the word 'October' of which I always liked the axe-like sound. A lousy damn month, said Ariane, really. A month where there's nothin' left to do . . .

In a few days my little sister Ariane would've been seventeen, we would've given her a gift. And this reminds me of this dream that had really troubled me in the first days that followed Ariane's departure. A strange dream, the first of all those that I'll never again have to tell her.

A little light-brown critter escaped from a package—a package that someone, I don't know who, is in the middle of unwrapping, I see scattered papers.—The critter runs on the table—or rather, under the table—which I turn over to chase it It's a little table Or a chair Or only some sort of wooden frame on wheels, and on it I clearly see the critter running and escaping being crushed.

Strangely, I feel that this bug belongs to someone—or in any case has a connection to—but I don't know to whom. My hunt, in itself, is not linked to the person in question, because I don't know that person: it is solely motivated by my horror of insects. The atmosphere is dry, anxious.

I'm not really sure what I'm trying to crush the critter with. I miss it several times, it's still running. As it abandons the corner where it was holed up to scurry across an open area (the floor, or some other indeterminate plane) I throw the object (it too is indeterminate) that I was holding in my hand at the critter and this time I don't miss.

I don't know if it's really me or someone else who turns over the crushing object (because there's still someone with me in the room   A woman whom I don't see clearly and who's maybe brunette but even that's not for sure)   or else if the thing turns itself over, either that it rolls, or else that it moves under its own power. The object, finally, is maybe really a hairbrush with metallic bristles. I threw it at the critter with the bristle side up, hence the momentary fear of having missed it again.

It always happens that it turns over and gives me the fleeting impression of a blue and black beetle literally burst, wide open, impaled on the prickles of a sparkling thistle   Blue   blue   blue   The unbearable crackling blue of Abel's eyes.

Several days after Ariane's departure, Clara gave birth.

I leave the maternity ward in a state of internal splitting rather akin to total absence   I see myself look   act   take the bus   I see myself even from several positions at the same time, but inside my head there is absolute emptiness.

Getting off the bus, I practically knock into a young pregnant woman before whom I mechanically move aside and who falls into my arms:

—Camille! Jeez, Camille, don't you recognize me?

—Mylene!

—Oh, I'm so happy! Can you believe . . .

I pull her a little away from that bus stop where we are going to end up causing a ruckus, by dint of blocking folks from getting on and off. There's a storm wind blowing dust in our faces making whirlwinds of old bus tickets down on the ground. She had come to make peace with her mother, but Gertrude wouldn't even open the door for her.

— . . . Maybe she wasn't home . . .

—Oh, my eye, says Mylene, I know her well, my mother, and her mule-headed silences behind the door. She was there, I tell you.

I look at my shoes.

—Even bitches don't reject their pups, Mylene sniffles again in the bistro where I dragged her to get us out of the wind. That's not a mother, that I've got, it's . . . It's . . .

Patiently, I cheer up Mylene, as she expects me to. She must think of her child, as for the rest . . . Leave the past behind   Look towards the future and that whole business. It's true, it's true, agrees Mylene who's already started to resemble all the Mothers and in particular her own.

—And you? finally sighs Mylene at the end of a series of sobs.

I practically wipe the nose of this Gertrude the Second and what's more without malice. I say that things are fine. That I'm a school residence monitor. No sense troubling her with the incomprehensible complications of my existence. Besides she's going on about my mother who at least is a real mother . . . I say It's true It's true and I watch the door of the bar beyond which the storm intensifies in violence, whirling up the old tickets bottle caps Carambar wrappers to phenomenal heights.

—This weather! sighs Mylene. How's your brother?

I say that Abel is still the same, with his rifle and his boots, he's gotten enormously fat, that he stalks the street in silence.

—Poor boy, says Mylene. He isn't really normal . . . And your younger sister?

—She left.

—I know, says Mylene, but since then . . .

—No, she hasn't come back yet. She's pregnant.

—Huh?

—That's what she told us . . . Do you realize that last year she was still juggling with her balls?

—Ooh la la, says Mylene sucking down the contents of her glass. When I think that I didn't even have the right to play . . . And it's your little sister who ran off. Me, if she hadn't thrown me the fuck out, I never would've left . . .

I order another milk with grenadine for Mylene, this one's on me, and another tea with lemon for me, just to give myself something to be nauseated about. I'm waiting for Mylene to have collected in her already-considerable belly enough encouragement to keep on living for a bit. And while waiting, I chat as I learnt to do so well around the Mothers.

Girl or boy, Mylene won't flip out either way, wisely weighing the advantages of one and the other to fairly come to a tie. I approve. The essential thing, ain't it true, is that it shouldn't want for anything . . . I agree again. The tea with lemon upsets my stomach a little more. I sweat. When Mylene smiles at her future infant unspoiled and pure, she looks so much like Gertrude it's striking.

—Do you remember . . . says Mylene becoming serious again and enveloping me in her gaze with a sort of gentleness that's looking for somewhere to land, of faint apprehension or nervousness Remember? . . . Her sombre gaze locking itself onto mine, awakening there the lost echoes of another gaze, that of Gertrude when she promised me the Black Forest, and I feel myself slipping slightly. Do you remember when you used to send things up to me in the basket?

—Your little sister was the one who had the most on the ball, says Mylene, but it was you who was my favourite . . . I really liked you, you know.

I wrack my brains for a way to get her away from that window (which will lead her back yet again to the unfairness of her mother) without riding roughshod over her tender feelings. But I'm worried over nothing, because Mylene moves on to a whole other idea:

—Guess what I'm gonna call it?

—Mmm . . . That makes two first names to guess, right.

—No, says Mylene laughing, only one: I'll call it Camille. It's pretty, Camille, and it ain't common . . .

I don't remember what else we said besides that with Mylene. I remember that I had to rush to the bathroom to throw up the tea with lemon. Mylene said that   My goodness! By any chance might I, also, be . . . ? I reassured her on that point, before abandoning her once and for all in the high wind that was gusting up torrents of dust.

I can still see the image of the baby all red and wrinkled sleeping next to Clara. It's a girl. Clara's gaze, calm and pacified, slips into mine with the sort of flexibility as a lucky, silky thing. I smile back at her, and she opens the package.

—Did . . . Did YOU make this?

As if stunned, she manages to unwrap the embroidered bib that I crafted a while back in Home Ec sewing class. It's white, embroidered with a range of colours from pale pink to dark purple, sumptuous like the linens of a princess, shimmering with threads interwoven torturously, with a manic regularity. Demented embroidery By-product of Flamboyant Gothic style A true cry of panic that no one understood—the teacher couldn't deny that that was my work, because I had embroidered it in class. My mother couldn't deny it either, having bought the thread with me. However they both looked at me as if there was a ghost standing behind me. They congratulated me, with the respect due to monsters who are seized by an unexpected stroke of genius.

I buried the object at the bottom of a box, in a shroud of tissue paper, never for one instant imagining that I would ever have use for it. The teacher had said It's an odd design for a bib, still though, technically, I can't give you less than an A . . . You ought to embroider altar cloths for the cathedral instead. As everyone knew my opinions, about the clergy as well as about embroidery and other tasks for 'young ladies', the whole class had a good laugh. But this masterpiece of despair awaited its destination: it only lay a couple of years in its cupboard.

—You made it? Really?

Clara's eyes opened beneath me like chasms.

—Yes.

—Her name is Camille, said Clara taking my hands in hers and squeezing them very hard. What do you think of her?

Camille, it surely wasn't 'common' in the neighbourhood, but it was going to end up that way. If my little sister Ariane comes back, if Mylene doesn't move, in a few years who will still remember, when I've disappeared somewhere in the wide world, that I was the origin of this epidemic?

Afterwards, with Ariane's little Camille, I had a hard time pulling myself back together. I had the extravagant impression that I had made babies with everyone, to such an extent that my own existence is deserting me, beginning to float away, dispersed in several contradictory images, without anchor, without reality . . .

The Mothers ought to have killed themselves, if only from fatigue. But no They wandered in limbo between the morning fog and the mean little evening wind that would go into their necks like the blade of a knife. They stepped over puddles of grey water and went home to stir the stew Happy as girls at their First Communion when the sun shone on Easter, that worn out sun in our neighbourhood that smells of mud from the gutter. Then they would lift up their heads toward the clouds, taking a deep breath, and looking at us, us kids, become suddenly gigantic, bigger than them, as inscrutable as a crowd of statues, and resembling That Man or That Woman in a distant and gloomy manner.

Me, I resembled no one And my mother secretly cherished my singularity, like a vague promise of revenge for the petrification of the passing years. She began to say When you have your bachelor's . . . as she would have spoken of a crown, of a brilliant jewel on my forehead, for her very own triumph. But at the same time she would watch over me from the corner of her eye, like a too-pretty vase that might lack a steady base.

I still have in my nerves, in every fibre of my body, that discreet and almost invisible surveillance ceaselessly directed at me by my mother. She would say nothing to me, or things of little importance, taking my waist or the nape of my neck in the curve of her arm as if to keep me from getting lost, propping up my whole body then as if I were suddenly about to fall As if she saw me teetering too close to the void.

In reality, even though I feel in general pretty steady on my feet, I must admit that it's not at all any more the same equilibrium that was expected at the outset. My mother knew that without anyone needing to tell her. And today I wonder: does one have the right to change one's sense of equilibrium?

This is a question that I didn't ask myself at the time, because, as Ariane would say, I always ask questions afterwards, it's more comfortable and more reliable, and otherwise you don't make any progress.

But 'afterwards', that becomes very quickly a little too late Everyone is already looking at you sideways and is that really the time to examine yourself from within when you're expected to prove, right there on the spot, that you're really still the same The one everybody's used to That you had neither changed nor deviated nor denounced nor betrayed even though everything demonstrates the opposite That you didn't go over 'to the other side' That you still know where the borders are, and know on which side you have to stay . . .

My mother—the suspicion occurs to me—was maybe verifying I was still present, in these fits of physical proximity. And if I never pushed her away, like Abel would do later, it was less out of tenderness or instinctive understanding than out of prudence, hypocrisy, conscious as I was of the inexorable growing gap.—Something that I never wanted. Never. I'd like to shout it to everyone.—

It was already much too late, and I'm ready to admit that my mother had understood it well before me: almost without words, almost without reproach, already she was looking for me in the dark.

Then there grows in me a rage, a vast temptation to massacre as one has in fits of delirium, and I break my back trying to explain to OTHERS, to those who don't give a shit, and who slap me on the back and laugh their heads off, to what extent this world is upside down To what extent I see it To what extent I would like to wreck it all, reduce it to ashes—*tabula rasa*, as they say, and they even sing it—To what extent I don't want to change, I don't and will not change!

—No one, said Ariane perched on her heels and lifting again the sides of her vast skirt to play the butterfly, NO ONE can know how much I will not change!

She was talking of something else, of her destructive yen for living, but I finally deduced from this that obsessions are our birthright, it's more or less in the family, and that we carry the torch of life and of carnage with equal stubbornness.

So my mother shrugged one shoulder or the other, obeying Ariane's exhortations advising her to switch them up, having humbly learnt moreover that everything wears out, even the ferocious appetite of young girls. But what if she were wrong after all?

Around me, in my other realms, they laugh. They say Ah ah! Anti-establishment . . . And it's true that it's becoming fashionable among the children of the bourgeoisie—And that it will pass, because it almost always passes—But I'm not having a delayed adolescent identity crisis. I snuck on board that boat, without the necessary papers. And since they can't throw me overboard, because they have scruples, they let me continue the journey despite my bad manners.

Doesn't stop them from keeping an eye on me, one way or another: I'm not a 'real' anything. Besides I will never again be a 'real' anything, anywhere. Not among my own kind, not among the others. From now on I have one foot on either side of the border, and I won't budge, no matter what conviction or force they may use to push me or pull me over to the nice side where there are bluebirds and flowers. Badmouthing slang and mastering the pluperfect of the subjunctive, I'll keep my traitor's mouth. The only thing that remains with me from before, like an ugly little suitcase.

Back home, I will have to say in my defence that I didn't really choose, it happened to me by surprise. One day while I was looking out the slitted window to distract myself, I had my insides illuminated by some books. Can one shut one's eyes again once they've been opened to the light? They'll understand. They also like rainbows.

To the others, I will endlessly give voice to, always and forever, my anger. That rage that grabs you in your gut when you find yourself somehow thrown on the other side of the pane, from where you're able to watch, and if worse comes to worst to participate in, your own destiny.

I framed myself in a two-way mirror. On this side, one sees One understands One knows One foresees. One might even become a 'Great Man', with just the tiniest little bit of luck . . .

On the other side of things, one continues to see nothing but one's own minuscule reflection. And I as much as I've tried to signal to them, they've already lost me a little, I can tell by their hesitant or closed look when we meet in the street.

Here, they speak to me politely. Without hollering. Saying 'we' and not 'me 'n you' And I respond in a sensible voice Of course Obviously and Don't you think, in this way I play at the indispensable comedy that renders me tolerable. But I don't deceive them any more than is necessary. With I don't know what coarseness of gesture or look, with I don't know which tiny clashing of an outfit which I chose with care—or worse yet: with that air of being all dressed up in my Sunday best invariably given away by an accessory bought on impulse and much too elegant for me—they catch me out. Become cautious. Heap on me their sympathy their understanding . . . They're always a little too nice with me, as if I had suffered a lot or was very 'deserving' as my mother would say.

Then I'm much more brutal than usual, while on this fine side of the mirror, in this sanctuary, the best ones rejoice at my coming, exactly as the ones back home, from the other side, forgive me for already being a little gone.

—That's not how it's supposed to be, complained Ariane, just before her romance novel phase. Look, mom, when you're a kid, there's never a problem with the pick-up: You meet some kid who seems nice, you say to 'im Wanna play? There's no strings attached, it's direct. If he don't like you, he says no and you tell 'im he's a show-off or a dumb jerk. If he asks you Play what? It's because he's cautious but not hostile. If he says that his mother don't want 'im to, he's a weirdo or a scaredy-cat. And if he says yes right away, you know that he likes you a lot too and that's a pal for life.

—Whereas now, grumbled Ariane, honestly what a loada shit! The girls put on airs with you, the boys look at you like you were three rungs below them, and if you let a guy get near you, you become his property just like that His ice-cream cone. The little flower in his buttonhole . . . Anyway, you can't talk to anyone any more! You think that's normal, do ya?

My mother lifted a shoulder, almost always the same one, looked at Ariane in confusion, answered that after all she wasn't wrong, but what can you do . . . Ended invariably by recommending that she go out with a few of her girlfriends To beware of boys, and especially of 'creeps' in general much older ones who sniffed around young gals And to . . . to . . . to . . . , immediately reintroducing that notion of latent danger that annoyed Ariane so much.

That Richard with his cow eyes, with his travelling-salesman crude sense of humour, shouldn't even have had the ghost of a chance with Ariane. Nor any Don Juan from the neighbourhood, with or without wheels. How was Ariane seduced? But my mother, Mylene, the Mothers, had they been 'seduced'? Of course, if you consider that among us 'seduced' means being led into getting pushed around, to being convinced by being worn down, taken and carried off like a parcel into a life that one can't choose in any case, since it's not an informed choice. So the first guy who makes nice . . . Especially if one let oneself be dragged like a dope into his bed . . .

But Ariane, no. Ariane dug her heels in the way others blow their brains out. Ariane will never forgive me.

And me I stay framed in the mirror, watching all that, and realizing finally that when you flee a wasteland, you ought to be able to take everyone else along. Otherwise it's not worth it. It doesn't change a Goddamn thing in this world.

Now it's been two years since Ariane stormed out slamming the door. And about a year and a half since Clara left in turn. I remember: it was in October.

Since forever, the dentist had had an annoying little chronic cold and vague intentions of pulling up stakes that Clara would combat with passivity and silence. He used as a pretext the baby's first sneeze to bring back on the table that famous South so luminous, so healthful for children . . . So . . .

Telling me this Clara didn't look at me Was looking out the window or, rather, towards the crib And you understand, deep down . . .

They sold the house on the cliff, I don't know what he had against that house, except that maybe it was easier to sell than the other one . . . So much the better. I won't be able to go there any more to dabble with even the least memory. They left the city, hiring an agency to sell the house with the office that has been closed ever since, blind and deaf like a tomb.

Sometimes, I pass by, with my scooter, revving the motor as if it were a cry from my gut. If I didn't have a mother, I would drive full speed into the stucco facade that's become all rundown by dint of the rain and neglect. That would make a big bloody smear that would take the place of the sun.

But I have a mother—or just a good excuse for the cowardice that's in me like a heavy pool—so I continue to hit the books in order to have a jewel on my forehead, of which she can go on being innocently proud for the rest of her miserable life.

Clara writes to me frequently that Camille is doing well. Drools. Smiles. Babbles. Crawls on all fours. Stands up. Runs around. Talks. That the house with the office is sold. That she will come back to finish moving out. That on this occasion we could see each other again, if I'm free. That she'll introduce Camille to me, you'll see how cute she is. How are you, Camille? Your studies? Your life? All my love. Lots.

I respond just as frequently that my studies are going along. Rather well. My life too, really. That my little sister is not coming back. That my brother is still the same, the neighbourhood too. That I wish her. That I hope that. That I will surely be free, she just has to let me know as soon as she knows the dates. That I'm sending all my love.

I tried so hard to talk it out with her. To shed light, even a little, on what had happened between us and that dissolves like a dream . . . She doesn't know. Doesn't answer. Or answers that she doesn't know, it's complicated . . . Once again it's a question of memory, as if implicitly, under the seriousness of my letters, she didn't dare detect anything but this obsessive fear: of forgetting. She assures me that she never forgets me. Will never forget me. Ever. And as for me I have the impression of having been once and for all laid out in her head and covered with a big white sheet.

I spin my wheels. I extricate myself patiently from grey days, one after another, like sticky sheets. There are more and more of them, with no certainty that there's anyone left underneath them.

The days when I have free time and energy to burn, I go biking with Abel along the canal. We roll for hours, until our eyes are frozen by the cold sky. And we never say a word between us, even during breaks, while we snack sitting in the reeds.

My brother is a menhir possessed by a turbulent and secret life, probably indecipherable to himself, and that never shows except in his eyes, in flashes or unpredictable sparks. He never communicates with anyone, he still has no friends, not even a girlfriend or a crush. As if this void that he has always had more or less around his body only gets deeper with the years, taking on the proportions of a desert where he can be seen petrifying till the end of time.

He refuses to see other doctors, to swallow other drugs He refuses more and more often to wash, to go to work, to get up, even. He refuses everything. He stares at the wall of his room for hours, stricken at the least contact with that silent howling that makes everyone recoil, one hand strangling the other with frightening cracking noises . . . Abel is truly frightening now when he looks you in the eye.

And when he stares at nothing, all stretched out, his eyes closed upon some absence, he's sad like a dead dog.

There . . . , had said Clara, her black gaze tense like a wind-filled sail, containing God knows what memories, what impulse, which ought to have stayed contained.

All the same it makes me happy to see you again . . . You haven't changed, Camille, you . . . It's true that it hasn't been that long . . .

At the height of her thigh, and thirty years younger, the same black eyes, immobile, were considering me seriously. I was suffocated by the resemblance: a miniature Clara, stuck to the legs of the real one, hesitated to smile at me.

—She's sleepy, said Clara. Things will go better once she's slept. Shall we go to bed, baby?

—Ya.

—Yes, says Clara. Ye-es.

—Yya!

—Pigheaded, says Clara joyfully. She talks, but she has her own language, there's nothing to be done for now. A truck, it's a dolla, and a dolly is a didi. Pppp . . . So, off to bed.

—Yya, says Camille with a smile as sudden and full as that of the original, to bed!

The baby put to bed, we don't have anything more to say to each other. Clara smiles at me in silence, from the other side of the table.

—You're doing well, Camille?

—Yes.

Silence.

—You want some tea?

—No.

— . . . Something else?

—No.

Clara's gaze falls back on her folded hands. I would have thought, says Clara, that this would be easier. In letters . . . It's true, says Clara, that you were never very chatty.

Camille . . . , says Clara with a very great gentleness, as if she were pulling aside a veil or my hair to uncover my true face. I thought a lot about you, you know . . . It's good that we can still write to each other, not to lose touch completely . . . It's good that you exist, says Clara with that look that seems to be filled up from the inside by something that's being held back. I'm happy that you came. That you're there.

And later, while we tied up boxes to do something finally: Don't be sad . . . I shrugged my shoulders, and the string broke between my fingers.

Then the child began to cry in the bedroom. She had to get her up, change her, give her something to eat. Once again, she was very gay, and not at all intimidated any more. She sucked on my cheek willingly, and asked me to take her for a walk.

—Okay, said Clara, we'll go out.

—No. Ca-ille.

—You want to go with Camille?

—Ya.

—Without Mama?

—Ya.

—You're sure?

—Ya! Not you.

—You're not going to cry? Listen, afterwards you're not going to cry?

—No!

I said Stop worrying her like that will you, I'm perfectly capable of taking a baby for a walk, what are you thinking?

—For several weeks now, says Clara, she goes crazy like this with people . . . But don't go too far . . . It never lasts very long: after, she wants to come back, quick, quick . . .

I say Of course That I would have anticipated something like that. And Clara's look, briefly hidden, surrenders again its entire surface Black veil fitted everywhere Resistant to the driving wind.

While we wrap Camille in her woollies, Clara smiles again with a vague sorrow, asking me if I really don't mind, in the end going back to tying up boxes as if I had somehow punished her.

I take a walk with Camille, who follows me as best she can lifting her knees very high to take big steps. Seized by remorse, I slow down a little, but now she's dragging me along. It's a game. We make our soles click together.

When a truck passes, she sticks out a finger:

—Dolla!

I say no, truck. I sit her on a low wall, so that her face is level with mine:

—Tru-ck.

—Ya, says Camille in that conciliatory tone that she's already pinched from grown-ups, Ya . . . Do-lla!

She smiles at me as if she were giving me something, and looks around, methodically, the length of the street. A little farther along next to the sidewalk, she spies a small blue truck parked. Emergence of the little finger, pointed, stiff:

—Dolla!

I don't react, lost in contemplation of her great black eyes that don't blink. That taunt me good-humouredly.

—Do-lla!

This baby looks so much like her mother that the tiny little blade in me turns over, that I am blinded by pain for a fraction of a second—last little bubble of a cadaver that we'll finally finish drowning.—

—That? Says Camille whose little pointed finger suddenly jabs in my eye. That?

—Oh yeah! That's what's waiting for you, doll, what do you expect? That . . . That . . . What am I getting myself into?

The big dark eyes stare me down, with an extraordinary fondness. And little Camille, after patient reflection, finally offers me, as if that resolved everything:

—Tr-ck?

Then, as if there were suddenly a desert around her:

—Mama?

I brought the child back to her mother, once and for all. Because it is absolutely out of the question that I fall in love with the second generation TOO, shit!

We tied up some more boxes, Camille tangling up a hank of twine to her heart's content.

—You know . . . One day I stole a flower from you. I really ought to tell you . . .

—Oh really? said Clara who was looking for the scissors and who suddenly turns around to smile at me.

—Yes. It was a long time ago.

Her sombre gaze is on me, suddenly relaxed as if by a calming of the wind.

—I find that unbelievable, says Clara, stealing flowers . . . I would have given them to you, in any case. If only it had occurred to me, if only you had asked me for them . . .

—Not 'some', one. I was cheated, anyhow. It was fake.

—Serves you right, says Clara as if finally she had found a way to say what was weighing on her mind, all you needed was to have confidence. What do you mean, fake?

—Fake. Artificial. Plastic and feathers. Aren't you ashamed?

—Me? Artificial flowers? No, you . . .

—Yes, you did. It was in the waiting room . . .

—Hmph, says Clara. The waiting room . . .

— . . . and I was twelve or thirteen.

—Huh? Says Clara completely letting the packing twine fall. What are you talking about?

—The day with Ariane, with her tooth. The flower, I had stashed it in the marble bag. It was for a girl.

Clara laughs right in my face A silent laugh, thrown as if by a movement of her entire body.

—What a joker, that Ariane . . . I bet that it was her idea! By the way, do you have any news?

I say no, no news. That I had been scared stiff . . . It's simple, I never dared tell you about it.

—You're becoming very bold, said Clara with a lift of her smile.

—But how silly you are, says Clara with her hands suddenly in my hair, I would have given it to you, I assure you . . . What a story.

I take her hands away from my hair. With gentleness. With firmness. Her gaze on me, swollen like a sail, that stretches near the edges, and finally gives way.

—She was pretty, at least, the girl?

—Not as pretty as the flower . . . You realize, it was the most beautiful flower that I'd seen in my life, and it didn't exist.

Clara's gaze that once again rushes to meet mine, tensed, almost vibrating That's going to flinch That flinches:

—You see very beautiful things everywhere, says Clara, that don't exist . . .

Sudden jolt of the gaze, as if moved by shifting but light winds, as if in imperceptible distress or nostalgia.

— . . . But they're wrong, says Clara. They ought, OUGHT TO HAVE been as you see them . . .

—Camille . . . , says Clara, after a tiny little silence in which we watch without reacting the other Camille sucking on the twine. You know, Camille . . . In one way or another, they did more or less exist all the same . . . Don't you think?

—No.

—Camille, we don't eat that, look here. Give to Mama.

—Yes, says Clara whose gaze, when she gives it back to me, has very lightly superficially sunk but immediately stretched again. Yes, they existed. Even if . . . You can't have a memory of something that never was . . .

The memory again The thing fully horizontal under the white sheets. I said exactly. I had no memory.

Her gaze then hid with stupefying speed, as one dodges a blow that one doesn't intend to return.

Fortunately, she didn't repeat her stupid 'I ask for your forgiveness', because I really think that I would've slapped her, just to clear out the memories in question.

Where I come from, disgrace held its head high and kept an insult on the tip of one's tongue, which is as good a way as any to live with it.

Asking forgiveness, it's really a bit naive: why not ask too, while you're at it, for comfort and an acquittal?

On the way back, I got smashed, on the off chance it would brighten my mood. I also sang, to cheer myself up.

'The chiiiil-dren of the Earrrr-th
Don't give a shit about God
La la la la la laire . . .
How they looo-ve each other the lov-ers . . . '

Oh Ariane Ariane if you knew.

But it doesn't cheer me up, and there was no more Ariane. Just Abel who was hanging around, pale as an unlit street lamp.

The sky was so grey that it made me think of the canal. I suggested getting out the bikes, that or something else.

The wind was soft against my face. Humid and soft like a cold sheet that one can't shake off any more. I had a hard time pedalling, I was still a little drunk. Finally I suggested we take a break.

I gave some gingerbread to Abel who's always hungry. And also some coffee, that I had filled a Thermos bottle with as usual. Above the unmoving canal, the whole sky went on by in an imperceptible shifting. I don't know what I did wrong, the coffee was practically cold. It was foul. I sang again:

'The lo-verrrrs of Haaaa-vre . . .
Have no neeed . . . o' the seeeea'

—That's Ariane's song, said Abel. Stop.

—It's a regular song. La la la la . . . la la la . . . La la laaa . . . La la laire . . .

—Stop! shouted Abel standing above me stuffing his two hands very quickly in his pockets. Then he looked like he was forcing himself to do something, and ended up moving stiffly away to the edge of the reeds.

—Where you going?

— . . . To piss, Abel tossed off towards me with a snarl over his shoulder.

I've been waiting for him for several minutes, gathering the papers, putting together the Thermos and the flask, tracking down anything that might still be lying about, the Opinel knife, the lighter . . . When I raise my head, the insidious shifting of the clouds suddenly upsets my stomach.

And all of a sudden, without my having heard him come back, Abel is there again, above me And I don't know why I began to scream A crazy howl Of a murder victim.

In Abel's gaze that's on me, incandescent, I see the unbearable universe that is contained in his skull burn sizzle explode I see his immense fingers begin to wring themselves, all of his muscles swelling in place, and I have the absolute certainty that this time he's not going to fall over backwards but is going to throw himself on me still crouched down gathering up our stuff on the edge of the canal.

Springing madly, I throw myself head first and with my arms around my head into the reeds whose cracking fills the inside of my skull. Abel, carried along by his own momentum, is swallowed up in the roar of the waterfall with an immense splash.

When I finally pull myself together, so bruised and terrorized that the sky seems to topple into the canal, Abel has disappeared. There's nothing on the surface except for some big grey bubbles, that I can't stop staring at as they spin in concentric eddies and burst one after another, while the sky continues to tremble, as though viewed through water.

Much later, I saw Abel's body resurface in the canal with a light swaying movement and drift very slowly towards the drawbridge. I didn't call out. There was never anyone on the banks of the canal. I tied the sack on my bike, and I left.

Abel had never wanted to learn how to swim. Besides he had surely passed out. As for me, I barely know how to stay afloat. But what does that have to do with anything. I didn't think of any of that while I was watching my brother die Without a cry Without lifting a finger to bring him help Without the slightest internal quiver. In me there was nothing left Except flatness Greyness The smooth water of the canal like an immense shard of mirror reflecting nothing but the colourless day, absence, emptiness.

When I awoke from this strange numbness, I knew that I would never be afraid again. Ever. Of anyone. That the fear had come from Abel, radiating from him, contaminating anyone who approached him. That we were going to live in peace. That maybe Ariane would come back. But that was another form of delirium.

Then I realized that if he fell forward, this one time, it was doubtless due to the slope. The tears didn't come until later, when I remembered that he still had his fly open. Because they were going to fish him out like that, his naked penis cutting through the cold water, like one of those 'dirty old men' that my mother always feared.

Of course, it isn't even worth waiting any longer: my little sister Ariane will never call back. I always latch onto unimportant details, like that first name, that she had hung on her child because it popped into her head Out of habit To attach the name to someone else, in order to make it stay in place, to give it a recipient who wouldn't be me. Or else maybe like you plant a flower on a grave, *in memoriam*.

Someone is coming up the stairs, slowly, behind my back. Someone heavy, I hear their feet thumping up the steps.

Someone died today, that much I know. Or yesterday Or will die tomorrow. The dead pile up around me without me being able to tell if I'm one of them, because some of them are still standing. The dead are pulling me by my sleeve, to remind me of dim duties forgotten along the way and that I MUST remember.

Where then are the people from back home? What have I done with my little sister Ariane? And what did I do with Abel, my brother? What could I have done with them, I ask myself this, that is, if it really was up to me to take care of them, and what? To count them, to look after them, to make sure they're still there . . . To lead them, maybe, but how, but where?

And if it's not up to me to answer, then who is it up to? Who, I wonder. Because there's no one here but ME, and here has been for a long time on the other side.

Roquebrune, April '87.